**W9-DJC-277**

# Devin Rhodes Is
# DEAD

Jennifer Wolf Kam

# Devin Rhodes Is
# DEAD

Mackinac Island Press

*for the love of reading*

To my parents, with much love and gratitude

A Mackinac Island Book
Published by Charlesbridge
85 Main Street
Watertown, MA 02472
(617) 926-0329
www.charlesbridge.com

Library of Congress Cataloging-in-Publication Data
Kam, Jennifer Wolf, author.
  Devin Rhodes is dead/Jennifer Wolf Kam.
    pages cm
  Summary: To most people Cassandra and Devin are teenage girls who are best
friends—but Cassandra actually resents the arrogant and bossy Devin, and when
Devin turns up dead in a ravine Cassandra is wracked by her guilty secret.
    ISBN 978-1-934133-59-0 (reinforced for library use)
    ISBN 978-1-60734-752-1 (ebook)
    ISBN 978-1-60734-706-4 (ebook pdf)
1. Best friends—Juvenile fiction. 2. Murder—Juvenile fiction. 3. Guilt—Juvenile
fiction. [1. Best friends—Fiction. 2. Friendship—Fiction. 3. Murder—Fiction.
4. Guilt—Fiction.] I. Title.
PZ7.K12658De 2014
813.6—dc23                    2013033435

Printed in the United States of America
(hc) 10 9 8 7 6 5 4 3 2 1

Display type set in FG Noel and Blue Century
Text type set in Sabon
Printed by Worzalla Publishing Company in Stevens Point, Wisconsin, USA
Production supervision by Brian G. Walker
Designed by Susan Mallory Sherman

# Devin Rhodes Is DEAD

# AFTER

DEVIN RHODES, MY BEST FRIEND, is being buried in her parents' garden, two feet beneath the agapanthus, in a green ceramic urn. Just her ashes, really: charred little flakes of humanity, which bear no resemblance to her thick honey curls, faded jeans, and shimmering brown lip gloss. But she loved flowers. And while her mother's rows of budding shrubs are nothing compared to the lush gardens in Eastland Park—her favorite spot—this patch of moist, warm earth seems a fitting resting place.

Devin died over the weekend. And here's the thing: it's my fault.

Mrs. Rhodes lowers Devin's ashes into the fertilized earth.

"Good night, sweet girl," she says softly. She covers her face with her hands. Mr. Rhodes kneels beside her and pulls her toward him. They sob together quietly.

I stand slightly to the left of them. A warm sting settles into my eyes, and I feel a gorge in my stomach opening up wide. It seems impossible to imagine that the vast space Devin filled with her small, curvy body and much bigger personality is now empty. When we're fifteen, the world is supposed to be opening up to us, like the flowers that will soon bloom above

Devin. But Devin's world is gone, and without Devin, mine has closed up and shrunk beneath me.

Of course Devin's parents don't know it was my fault—my fault that her broken body was found at the bottom of Woodacre Ravine. If they knew, I wouldn't be standing here with them, watching them lay their only child to rest. The Rhodeses don't know, will never know. Only I can say for sure what happened between Devin and me—what led to all of this. Well, only Devin and I can say, which means that my secret is safe for as long as I can keep it. I grab onto the best-friend charm around my neck. It feels cool between my fingers, as it should.

Mrs. Rhodes stands up and turns toward me, her face a patchwork of red splotches, her cheeks wet. She squeezes my shoulder but keeps her eyes on the tiny brown clumps of earth beneath us. "I'm glad you could be here with us, Cass," she says.

Inside of me a scream churns slowly and pushes its way toward the surface. But whatever force moves it that far, another stronger one silences it, catching it just shy of my throat, where it lies there—a large, sour lump.

I bite on my lip. "Thanks." Here I am, playing the loyal, grieving friend when really, really . . . Devin knew the truth. When they found her she wasn't wearing the charm. She'd cast it off somewhere before it happened. I clasp my hands together and squeeze until I can see the white peaks of bone on my knuckles.

"I don't know about this, Susan," says Mr. Rhodes,

standing up. He chews on a fingernail. "This doesn't feel right."

Of course not, I think. How can it? Everything about this yells wrongful death, which were actually the coroner's words.

"Please, Ben, stop." says Mrs. Rhodes. "Don't."

"Who does this, Susan?" asks Mr. Rhodes. "Who buries their daughter in their own yard?"

Mrs. Rhodes shakes her head. "Devin loved gardens. What better garden than ours?"

"Any garden, Susan," says Mr. Rhodes, shaking his head. "Any garden but ours."

He looks like Devin at that moment, his light hair the color of hers and his face creasing the way Devin's did when she was irritated. I turn away—it's too much.

Mrs. Rhodes frowns and pushes away a stray hair from her forehead. "Let's finish this, Ben," she says. "Let's please just finish this."

Mr. Rhodes sighs and kneels down again in front of the agapanthus. He covers the urn with dirt and smoothes the dirt with his spade. Mrs. Rhodes grabs my hand, squeezing my fingers, the ones that, only a few days ago, casually strummed a new song on my guitar. The ones that tremble now when I even think about playing my guitar. My hand rests limply in hers, hoping—no, praying—that she'll let go soon.

Mr. Rhodes puts down the spade and runs his hands over the newly replaced soil. He wipes his hands, stands up, and stares for a moment at his daughter's grave. "I guess that's it." The creases gone, his face is empty, unreadable.

"Yes, that's it, isn't it?" Mrs. Rhodes's eyes are rimmed in red, making their pale gray-blue color jump out even more, the way Devin's used to. She dabs at them with a tissue.

It's then that I feel something softly brushing up against my neck. Not a breeze, but something. Something cool and constant, like air, like breathing. The hair on the back of my neck rises and sways. I shrug and shake my head.

"Are you all right?" Mrs. Rhodes is staring at me, her swollen eyes barely open.

The feeling disappears, and I rub my neck with my hand. "Um, yeah," I mumble, straightening up. "It's nothing." Weird, though, definitely weird.

Mrs. Rhodes puts her arm around me, a gesture that under normal circumstances would bring comfort. Instead I prickle. Her touch shoots a dull, aching pain down my arm and back.

"Thanks." There's nothing else I can say. Nothing except: *I'm the reason we're here, Mrs. Rhodes.* But that's not going to happen.

Mrs. Rhodes runs her hand down the side of my head. "Such pretty, dark hair you have, Cass. You're so lovely inside and out." Her voice cracks and fades to a whisper.

I want to push her hand away. But I let her stroke my hair as I clench my fists and wonder what she's really seeing.

She pats my cheek. "All right, then. Let's go."

We walk together toward the house. Mr. Rhodes drags the spade behind him, and it thuds against the

4

flagstone walkway. *Tell them; tell them,* I hear with each clunk.

*No, no, no,* my heart thumps back.

"You'll see, Ben," says Mrs. Rhodes, momentarily drowning out the accusing spade. "It was the right thing to do. This way Devin's always nearby, always close."

Mr. Rhodes doesn't answer. He just keeps heaving air through his body.

"You agree, don't you, Cass?" Mrs. Rhodes looks at me, her eyes watering.

She doesn't wait for my reply, which is good, because my tongue has glued itself to the roof of my mouth. She turns away. "It's what Devin would've wanted."

"Devin would've wanted to be alive," says Mr. Rhodes.

Mrs. Rhodes grabs my hand again, and I choke on the scream that threatens to burst from my throat. I swallow again and again and again.

Mr. Rhodes drops the spade and reaches for his wife. "I'm sorry, sweetheart," he says. "I'm so sorry." He brings her toward him, and she finally lets go of my hand.

# Before

"WHAT ARE YOU THINKING ABOUT, CASS?" Devin was stretched out beside the large lilac bush in Eastland Park. Her shirt lifted up slightly, revealing her flattened, tanned stomach. A tiny naval ring reflected the sun.

I adjusted my own shirt, aware that it betrayed the rolls of soft flesh beneath it. No navel ring for me—it would definitely drown. "Can you believe we're almost sophomores?" I asked. "Only two weeks left as freshmen." My guitar, worn but strong, rested next to me. I'd played since sixth grade. It was old when I got it and had seen better days.

"Fresh*women*, Cass." Devin flipped over onto her stomach, her blue eyes wide. "Real high school—not the half-assed ninth-grade version where they keep us in a separate part of the school like we're infants." Devin's new persona: high-school bad girl. She'd been perfecting it all summer.

I laughed but only on the outside. "It wasn't that bad." I sat up and drew my knees to my chest, against my breasts, which continued to grow despite my nightly prayers to the contrary. "Tenth grade means more homework. I can wait for *that*." I uncurled and reached for the guitar. I'd just had it restrung. I strummed a little, plucking out a few notes to test the sound.

"Homework?" she said. "That's what you're thinking about?" She shook her head and laughed. "Rest up, Cass. This year we're going to have some real fun."

I continued to pick at my guitar. I'm pretty sure that whatever she had in mind was not my idea of fun.

"Are you listening to me?" asked Devin.

"Of course," I said, continuing to pick at the guitar. I loved the way it felt, the tautness of the strings, the way its curve fit perfectly onto my lap. "Listening but not agreeing," I responded.

The truth was I liked ninth grade. I liked being in the ninth-grade hall, wrapped in all that was familiar. I liked not being allowed in the student commons, where the older kids smoked. I liked not having to worry about who I might run into in the girls' room. Devin was my best friend, but there were some things I couldn't tell her. Not anymore.

"Cassandra Lorraine Kirschner," she said, sitting up. She studied me with those blue eyes. They were so light, so pale; they were almost like mirrors, too reflective. She shifted her weight to the side and leaned on her palm. "Are you scared of being in the big, grown-up halls?"

I looked up from the guitar. "No." I practically spat out the word. "Of course not." I hated the way she did that sometimes. The way she made me shrink into this tiny person she could shove into a box and stick into her jeans pocket, if her jeans weren't so tight.

"Don't be so sensitive." She smiled, her teeth white and straight and perfect. "Gotta grow up sometime, right, Cass-girl?"

7

"Uh, *yeah*," I said, tugging out a few blades of grass. "I saw the puberty movie in fifth grade, too."

She laughed, tilting back her head as if she were in a shampoo commercial. Her newest move. "You're funny," she said. "That's why I keep you around."

"Ha, ha." I smiled back, but I thought something very bad. I thought, or more, I wondered, what it would be like if Devin weren't around anymore. I didn't wish for it; I just thought about it. Thinking it was bad enough.

Devin didn't know this. I would never have told her, and lately, she hadn't been too interested in my thoughts. Sure, she asked me things, told me stuff, but it was just conversation. Small talk. Snippets of invisible nothings. It wasn't the way it used to be with us—when we told each other everything, stayed up late, lolled on the dry summer grass, stared up at the stars, shared our diaries. We were filling space—that's all. It didn't mean anything anymore.

"Lighten up, Cass. It'll be great." She pushed some blond hair behind her ears.

I tugged on more blades of grass. "I never said it wouldn't be."

She got up and plucked a lilac from the bush, then sniffed it and twirled it in her hand. "God, I love the way these smell."

Devin went on and on about tenth grade, as if I hadn't already made it clear that I didn't want to talk about it. I nodded a lot and raised my eyebrows and said, "Um-hmm." I threw in a few knowing smiles, too. It was like how our seventh-grade chorus teacher once told us that if we were too nervous to sing in the concert, we could mouth "watermelon" over and over again and it would look like we were singing even if our stomachs were tied in shoestring knots and our mouths tasted like cotton.

"And the guys in high school," Devin said, and whistled, which finally got my attention. I liked boys but hadn't dated yet, although I'd definitely thought about it. Devin had dated, if you could call what Devin did dating, though I didn't think anyone would. The ample rolls under my shirt might have been part of the reason I didn't date. Another reason might also have been Devin. It wasn't easy being her best friend, especially when guys were around.

"*Guys*, Cass, not boys," she continued, her pale eyes darting around like flecks of light. "Men almost. Can you imagine?" She chewed on her lip, the way she did when she talked about the opposite sex. I knew that look well—she'd been boy crazy since the fifth grade. Since Jared Tomassi kissed her in the woods behind school. It had been manageable for a while, but each year it had gotten worse. A string of wrong choices, bad boys, or "practice," as Devin called them. Stepping-stones until she reached Prince Charming or something like that. Devin went after boys with the same intensity she did everything. They loved it—and I got dragged along like an overweight pull toy.

Devin nodded and closed her eyes. "The guys are the best part of high school."

I placed the guitar gently back down on the grass.

Then I rolled over onto my stomach and faced her. My shirt had ridden up again, and the grass scratched at my skin. I didn't bother to fix it this time. "That's really all you think about, Devin, isn't it? Guys?"

Devin lay down again on her stomach and stretched out across from me. Our faces were close, and a soft spring breeze moved between us. Devin's lips curled into a smile.

"Mostly," she said. Her teeth were even whiter in the sun.

# AFTER

DEVIN'S PARENTS SIT SHIVAH at their yellow and white colonial a few blocks away from my own yellow and white colonial. Mrs. Rhodes isn't Jewish, but the Rhodeses were Rosenbergs once upon a time in Austria (says Mr. Rhodes), and shivah is how Jewish people mourn. The mourners tear their clothes, cover their mirrors, sit on boxes, and, well, eat. Usually there's smoked fish and *babka*. I know this because I'm a quarter Jewish, thanks to my grandfather.

My mother opts out with a migraine. "Send Susan my condolences," she says.

"Sure you don't want to come?"

She sighs, and there's a definite hint of melodrama. "I'm sure. I feel bad, of course, but she was your friend. I don't belong there."

Everyone belongs there, I think. Who doesn't pay respects when a fifteen-year-old girl dies? But then that's my mother. Since the divorce she avoids social obligations.

"Okay," I say.

"I'm sure Susan Rhodes will have plenty of company." She hands me a bakery box with a chocolate *babka* in it, and I leave.

Even though Devin was my best friend, our mothers never had much to do with each other. My mom's life

11

trajectory went south—her Perfect Life Mission failed. She hates happily married people. My father left the state almost two years ago, which nixed any opportunities for male bonding between our dads. Susan Rhodes's life will now never be anything close to perfect. My mother should realize that.

I glance at the garden, at the disturbed patch of dirt. Underneath is what's left of my best friend. I suck in some air and rub my hand on my pants. I ring the doorbell. It takes a moment, a long moment during which I almost turn around and run back home. But then Mrs. Rhodes greets me at the door. Her eyes are rimmed in smudged dark mascara. She's dressed entirely in black.

"Oh, Cass," she says, her voice strained into almost a whisper. "You're here." She puts her arm around me and leads me into the living room, as though I've arrived at a macabre dinner party.

I play with the bakery box string. It's the closest I've been in the past few days to a guitar string, which isn't close at all. I can't even think about playing—every time I try, it takes me back to that day. To the last time I played and what happened next. I tuck the bakery box under my arm.

Mrs. Rhodes turns me toward her guests. She clears her throat and says, "Cass Kirschner." Her voice doesn't carry; it's too drained, too hoarse. So only a few nearby hear her say, "Devin's best friend."

*Devin's best friend.* My ears burn, and I stand there, numb, as the guests murmur greetings. I thrust the *babka* at Mrs. Rhodes.

12

She tries to smile and licks a tear that's dribbled down her face onto her lips. Her eyes are tired. "Thank you, sweetheart." She removes the string and peeks inside the bakery box.

"It's a Jewish cake," I say.

"Yes, it is." She nods and clears her throat again. "Send my thanks to your mother."

"Sure."

She gently pushes the box toward me. "Please. Just leave it on the table." She swallows and dabs at her eye with a finger. "I'll be right back with a cake plate."

I place the *babka* on a nearby coffee table. Now what? My feet are planted to the dark chestnut floor. The house is filled with Sylvias and Morrises and smells like the fragrance department at Macy's.

A woman I don't recognize brushes past me. "Sit—have something to eat." She hurries off into the kitchen.

I walk a few feet and find myself staring at a tray of smoked fish, the centerpiece to a large assortment of food carefully arranged on a long table that's not usually there. For once the abyss in my stomach isn't looking to be filled with food, but I take a plate and a fork and obediently lift a few slivers of sable off the tray.

An elderly friend or relative of the Rhodeses frowns at me over the top of her red bifocal glasses, her head a helmet of bluish hair.

She turns to her friend. "Devin had such a lovely figure."

Something bubbles inside me, hot and acidic. Right, I think, because the only thing tragic about Devin's death is that she had a great figure. Worse still, the fat girl lives.

Mr. Rhodes moves past me toward the door. "Jim," he says to another arriving guest. "It's kind of you to come."

He's shaking hands with Mr. Cordeau from Cordeau Jewelers in town. The Rhodeses get all their jewelry from him.

"I'm so sorry, Ben," says Mr. Cordeau. He wipes a thick hand across a shiny forehead. "I don't even know what to say."

"Thank you," says Mr. Rhodes, although he barely looks at him. "Have something to eat, please."

"Oh, I'm fine," says Mr. Cordeau. "You just take care of yourself and the missus."

Mr. Rhodes is gone almost before Jim Cordeau finishes his sentence. I'm glad. Mr. Rhodes reminds me too much of Devin. Everywhere there are reminders of what I've done.

Some kids from school are across the room. I want nothing more than to avoid them, blend into the crowd. My heart prickles—Gina and Lizzy are there. Gina waves to me. We used to be a foursome—Lizzy, Gina, Devin, and me—but that ended forever ago. Or at least a few months ago, which really is the same thing. I can't actually believe that Gina and Lizzy are here, after everything. Jack and Samantha are new friends of theirs and dating each other, I think.

14

I walk toward them; I have no choice, really. Better this way. Better to act natural—as natural as I can be when everything about this is so unnatural.

Lizzy moves toward me first. "Cass," she says, shaking her head sympathetically, "I'm so sorry. I know you and Devin were still close."

*Close?* She has no idea. No idea how close two people are when one is responsible for the other's death. How entangled they become. "Thanks," I say. "It's really hard." That sounds so dumb, so shallow. But I'm not lying. Even though—well, I'm not.

Gina puts her arm around me, and I stiffen. "It's so awful," she says. "I can't imagine anything worse." There are genuine tears in her eyes. Lizzy and Gina are best friends, just like Devin and I were best friends. I know they're each thinking how devastated they would be if one of them were standing there mourning the other. They probably can't believe I'm even there, dressed, having a conversation, stuffing my face with fish. They probably notice how dry my eyes are.

"So do they have any leads yet?" asks Jack, pouring himself some soda.

"Nope," says Samantha. She takes a bite of a cracker, which she's slathered in port-wine spread. "Just another unsolved case."

I don't know Samantha too well. The thought of her talking about Devin like she's some crime statistic while cracker crumbs fall onto her baby-doll top makes me want to shove her face into the port-wine spread. I am loyal, if nothing else.

15

But I can't call more attention to myself, so instead I politely nibble on my fish. The piece of sable slides down my throat, leaving a salty aftertaste. Samantha and Jack look at me, probably wondering how I can shovel fish into my mouth when my best friend is dead.

"I mean obviously someone pushed her," says Samantha. "Or brought her down there, you know what I mean?"

"Cass, do you think? I mean, that night—" Gina looks at me, really looks at me, and I know what she's thinking. But the less I say, the better.

I shrug. "I don't know," I say.

"Let's hope they catch whoever did it, and soon," says Jack. He puts his arm around Samantha. "I don't want my girl out with some maniac running around." He squeezes her tight.

"Maybe it was an accident," says Gina. "Maybe she just, I don't know, *fell*."

"Right," says Lizzy, shaking her head of shiny black hair. "Devin accidentally fell into Woodacre Ravine in the middle of the night." She reaches for a cracker. "Why was she out there in the first place? She had to know better. Although with her, who knows?"

"Well, what happened after everything, Cass? Was she still upset?" Gina runs her hand over her chin. "Do you think she, you know, jumped?"

My heart pounds. I think over and over again about the last time I saw her, the last time Devin and I looked at each other, really looked at each other. The

16

last thing I read in her face. What was it? If only, *if only.* . . .

"Anything's possible," says Lizzy. "But I'm thinking not."

Samantha shivers dramatically, clearly for effect. "The whole thing creeps me out," she says.

Everyone nods, including me. "They'll catch the bastard soon enough," says Jack, running his hand through the ends of Samantha's hair. "They always do."

"How do you know it was a guy?" says Samantha.

"It's *always* a guy," says Jack.

"I can't believe it," says Gina, shaking her head. "I mean, we *just* saw her. We—" She starts to whimper, and it's painful to watch. Lizzy touches her shoulder, but me, I'm frozen, my fingers squeezing the fork. "I just hope"—Gina takes a deep breath—"I just hope she didn't suffer." Lizzy grabs onto her, and the two of them sob together. It's what best friends do.

Just then a familiar figure enters the room, and I swallow a gulp of air. He's in a blue button-down shirt and khakis, possibly for the first time in his life. The blue shirt looks incredible against his olive skin, and despite my pain, I get a tickle in my insides. He nods and shakes hands with Mr. Rhodes. Even though he'd never met Devin's family, it makes sense to me that he's here. That Marcus is here right now, because he was there that night with me. The night it all happened.

"Hey, Cass," says Lizzy. "Isn't that the guy from the mall? The one you were with? What's his name?"

"Um, yeah." I chew on my nail. "Marcus."

17

"I didn't know you had a boyfriend," says Samantha, stuffing more crackers into her mouth.

"I don't," I snap. Who cares if I'm rude? Samantha barely knows me anyway.

"Sor-ry," she says, rolling her eyes at Jack.

I want to see Marcus, so I can't help myself from watching him. It's like the first time I realized that I could watch him forever. Then—oh, God—from across the room our eyes meet and I'm back there—back in that moment when everything went wrong.

A pain, an awful pain, slams into my head. It thumps against me and spreads to my temples. The feeling grows, strengthens, and my head sinks. Instinctively, I grab onto the charm on my necklace.

# BEFORE

"WE NEED NEW CHARMS," Devin said. We were walking down Birchtree Lane in town, which for some reason was lined with elms and sugar maples.

"Why?" I asked. We were just going for a walk, and suddenly we're buying new best-friend charms.

"Because we threw out the old ones." Devin said it so matter-of-factly, as though we didn't also throw out our friendships with Gina and Lizzy, our friends since second grade. Tossed out like gum wrappers. Several weeks before we'd had the fight to end all fights.

"No way," I said. "I'm saving up for a new guitar." I was done with those charms anyway. They were a little juvenile, if you asked me.

Devin was nothing if not persistent. "Cordeau will cut us a good deal. Especially since," she grinned at me, "he likes my mom."

"Everyone likes your mom," I said. It was true. It was hard to be more likable than Mrs. Rhodes. Perfectly coiffed and made up, stylish even in sweats (although I'd never seen that) and kind as can be. Real-life storybook princess. My mother hated her.

"No," Devin said, grinning, "he *likes* her likes her."

"What are you talking about?"

"You know," she said, "he's always giving her those big eyes and getting a little too close. He practically drools when we walk into the store. '*Well, hello, Susan,*'" she said, mimicking Mr. Cordeau. "'*Don't think I have anything in my store as beautiful as you.*'"

"That's gross."

"Beyond," she said. "But true. Can you even imagine them—?"

I cover my ears. "La, la, la, la, la!"

She laughed and slapped me on the shoulder. "Okay, okay. It's repulsive—but definitely worth the discount. Besides," she said, grinning, "my parents will probably pay for the charms anyway."

I was uneasy, and I felt it everywhere. "We're getting the same ones?"

She looked at me. "Well, yeah."

"Don't you think that's a little weird?"

"Halves this time, *not* quarters." She put her hand on her hips. "Unless you want a third of it for your guitar. Or is the guitar your *best* friend?"

"You're so funny," I said. "Okay, fine." But then I added something: "I want the half that says 'Be Fri.'"

She wrinkled her eyebrows. "What difference does it make?"

I shrugged. "I just like it." I did. I liked the way it almost looked like "Be Free." Almost.

"Whatever," she said. "The important thing is that we ditched those two losers." She made a face and stuck out her tongue. "Thank God."

I winced at the word *losers*. "That's harsh." Gina and Lizzy weren't losers. They just weren't.

"You're not still upset about it, are you?" she asked.

"No." I sucked on my lip. "Don't you think it'll be strange once school starts? I mean, seeing them?"

"You are still upset."

"I didn't say that."

"You're not thinking of making up with them, are you?" She frowned. "You better not, Cass. You're not leaving me alone."

"Relax," I said. "I wouldn't do that." Actually I couldn't. I was pretty sure that after our fight, Gina and Lizzy would never speak to me again.

"Good," she said. "Don't be upset. You're lucky—you stuck with the right quarter of the friendship pie." She smiled, then linked her arm in mine. "*We're* lucky," she added, leaning against me. "Right?"

I was buoyed by her change of heart. It was a sign of the old Devin. The one I met at the first-grade cubbies. The one who shared her snacks with me and invited me to play with her dollhouse every day after school. She's the one I stuck it out with despite everything, because, well, that's what best friends did. I uncurled my hand.

"Come on," she said. "It'll be fun." And just like that we were off to see the jeweler.

We walked into Cordeau Jewelers, onto a soft blue carpet that was so plush our footsteps were silent. A gentle bell at the door sent Jim Cordeau, the jeweler, hurrying out.

"Devin Rhodes!" he said, smiling. He was large and friendly. His bald head glowed under the bright lights of the store. "How's your mom?"

Yup, totally gross. I shot Devin a look, and somehow she grinned with just the corner of her mouth.

"Well?" he said. "Does she love her tennis bracelet?" Mr. Cordeau had a lot of bracelets, too, thick and gold, which dangled from his wrists. I'd never seen a man his age with so much jewelry. I guessed that's what happens when you actually make the jewelry.

"You know my mother," said Devin. "She likes anything that glitters." And I swear, at that moment, Devin was sparkling, too.

Mr. Cordeau laughed—a big belly laugh, à la Santa Claus sans the beard. "She sure does," he said. "I've got some wonderful new pieces I think she'd like. Do tell her to stop by when she has a chance."

Devin shot me an I-told-you-so look. "I'll let her know," she said to him.

Mr. Cordeau smiled and leaned on the jewelry counter. "So, what can I do for you girls today?"

"We're looking for best-friend charms," said Devin.

Mr. Cordeau raised his eyebrows. "Didn't I make some of those for you last year?"

Devin nods. "We had to toss them," she said. "No offense, Mr. Cordeau, but the other two quarters were given to the wrong people."

Mr. Cordeau nodded sympathetically. "Jewelry is forever," he said. "Not so much friendships, eh?"

"We like the one we had before," I said.

"We just need it cut in half this time instead of in quarters," said Devin.

"Ah, of course," said Mr. Cordeau. He walked over to one of the glass counters, pulled out a tiny key from his pocket, and unlocked the door. He carefully lifted out two little gold half-moon charms. They were like tiny glittering pebbles in his giant hand.

"Perfect," said Devin.

"Remember, I get the half that says, 'Be Fri,'" I said.

Devin rolled her eyes but didn't say anything.

"Wait here while I get some chains for you to try on." Mr. Cordeau walked over to another counter, humming something familiar that I couldn't place.

"I'm so glad we're doing this," said Devin. She grabbed my hand and squeezed it.

"Me, too," I said. And, to my surprise, I was, a little. I'd missed the feeling of the cool chain around my neck. I still reached for it sometimes, and it was weird that nothing was there. It was weirder, though, that Gina and Lizzy were gone, too. But I couldn't buy them back at Cordeau Jewelers.

"Here we go," said Mr. Cordeau. He put mine on first. His hands were heavy on my neck, and he breathed in and out quickly through his nose. I imagined his forest of nose hair blowing in a musky breeze. "How's that feel?" he asked.

The chain was cool against my skin, as it always feels. A small part of me liked that Devin was so insistent about getting new charms. Part of me, though, felt a little like it was a dog collar: If Lost, Please Return to Devin Rhodes. "Good" was all I said.

Mr. Cordeau smiled. His smile was large like the

rest of him and spread across his face. "Excellent," he said. "Your turn, Miss Rhodes."

Devin grinned and held up her hair in the back. Mr. Cordeau walked behind her and gently pulled the chain on. "How's that, hmm?"

Devin did the shampoo commercial thing with her hair. "Fabulous."

Mr. Cordeau laughed loudly again. "Your mother's daughter!"

Ew and double-ew. I grinned at Devin, and she grinned back.

"Let's take these off and wrap them up," he said, reaching for my clasp.

"We want to wear them home." Devin looked at me. "Right, Cass?"

"Sure," I said. Why not?

"Alrighty, then," said Mr. Cordeau. "I'll ring you up and send you on your way." He made his way to the register. "Cash or charge, dear?" he said to Devin.

She smiled, showing her white teeth. "My mother said to put it on her account."

I nudged her. I knew she hadn't asked her mother. She ignored me and kept smiling at Mr. Cordeau.

He looked at the two of us. "Everything okay?"

Devin was smiling at me now, but her eyes said something else entirely.

"Yes," I said. "Everything's fine." I wasn't going to argue as long as I didn't have to pay for it. I was still three months away from having enough cash for a new guitar, which was like forever in high-school time.

"Lucky girls!" he said. "Soon enough your boy-

friends will be buying you all sorts of sparkly things."
He winked again.

Devin tilted back her head and laughed. "Not the
boys we know."

I shrugged and smiled. "Definitely not." Not for
me. Devin had a chance if she stopped going after
jerks.

"Too bad," said Mr. Cordeau. He worked on the
calculator. "Pretty girls like you." He used the plural,
but for a very, very quick second his eyes lingered on
Devin. He looked down so quickly, I wasn't even sure
she noticed. But I did. It was always Devin. Even with
an old bald guy like Mr. Cordeau.

"Here you go," he said, looking up again. "Wear
them in good health!"

"Thanks," I said.

"You're the best," said Devin.

"Oh, my pleasure," said Mr. Cordeau. "Be sure to
give my regards to your mom."

"Sure will," she said, then turned to me and stuck
her finger in her mouth in a gag-me kind of way. It
was impossible to not giggle.

Devin and I walked out of the store together. The
late summer sun beat down on us and warmed me
from the outside in. I got a jolt of good feeling, and it
lifted me. "You were right," I said. "I'm glad we got
these. They look good." And at that moment, it was
like it always had been, Devin and me, me and Devin,
best friends forever. For real.

"Better than a dumb guitar, hmm?" she said.

The feeling was sucked right out of me. "My

guitar is not dumb," I said. "Just because you don't play—"

"Sorry," she said. "I just mean this is pretty special—that's all."

"Fine," I said, still irritated. "Leave my guitar out of it."

When we reached the sidewalk, she stopped and shot her hand up across my chest.

"What?" I asked.

She faced me and put her hand on top of my gold charm. Her manicured fingers just barely scratched my skin, but her hands were warm and soft. "Best friends forever, Cass," she said, "means forever."

"I know."

She pressed down harder, her hand pushing at my heart. I took in a quick breath.

"Don't forget," she said. "Gina and Lizzy forgot."

I nodded and exhaled slowly. Devin's hand, still on the charm, moved with me.

# AFTER

My HEAD IS POUNDING. Marcus moves toward me, through the crowd. He holds up his hand.

"Cass," he says. He doesn't shout because it's a shivah, after all, so I pretend I don't hear him. Seeing him brings it all back; he has to know that. Doesn't it do the same for him?

I need to go. I need to get out of this room. "I'll be right back," I say to Lizzy and Gina.

"Where're you going?" asks Lizzy. "That guy Marcus is coming over here. Don't you want to talk to him?"

Gina pulls me close. "Are you okay?"

I turn away. I can only imagine what I must look like now, sweat beads popping up all over my forehead, crazy swirling cartoon eyes, maybe. Gina knew me well enough, once. I don't want her looking at me too closely.

I press my lips together. "I need to be alone for a few minutes."

"Of course," Gina says. She lets go of me but not before she says, "We're here for you, Cass. I hope you know that. Just because things didn't—"

"Thanks," I say. It's what people say at funerals. Gina's not a liar, but I think she'd take her offer and run, a marathon maybe, if she ever found out the truth about that night—the night Devin died. If she found out what kind of a best friend I really am.

I leave my plate on an end table and head quickly toward the staircase, I don't know why, but I need to go upstairs. I'm drawn there; my body moves as if I don't have a choice. I know Marcus is watching me—I can feel it—but I keep going.

"That's gotta totally suck," I hear Jack say.

"This port-wine spread is amazing," says Samantha.

"Cass." Marcus is right there, faster than I thought. "Wait up, okay?"

I don't turn around. "I need to do something," I mumble.

"I just want to talk," he says. "Don't you want to talk? Cass," he says. "Cass, please look at me."

His voice melts me. I turn around for a split second and catch a glimpse of him, his eyes and his teeth. "I can't."

"Come on, Cass, it's *me*."

*It's Marcus.* I know but still. "I can't," I say.

I turn away and head up the tall staircase that's so similar to my own, my hand skimming the polished oak railing. He puts his hand on the railing, but I move mine too quickly and the opportunity is lost. We do not touch. I keep going, and Marcus doesn't follow. That would just be weird, and I'm sure he knows it. Even desperation has its limits in civilized society. I feel him watching me, though, and I know he's still at the bottom of the staircase.

At the top of the stairs, the door to Devin's room is open. I forget almost completely about Marcus, and I run to it. But then I stop in the doorway. My heart pops. Devin's room is freshly cleaned. Her bed is neatly made with the pink patchwork quilt. Her makeup case sits on her desk, a stick of brown lip gloss poking out from inside, as though she's just gotten ready to go out. Posters of celebrity crushes in various stages of undress hang on the wall. Nothing is out of place. Nothing has changed. Then I see, placed carefully beside Devin's bed, her pink terry-cloth slippers, her favorites, worn smooth. She's had them for so long, they've molded to the shape of her feet.

"Devin." I move toward them. My heart brushes against my chest, and my body bristles. It's a strange sensation, not painful, but not exactly pleasant. I don't know why but I say, "Devin?" as if I expect her to answer. "Devin?"

I was just here. *We* were just here. It was a night like a million others before it; we got dressed, put on makeup, talked about what might happen, told jokes. *Jokes*. But then that night wasn't like any other, because it was Devin's last. Just like that, any day can be your last. Everything we did that night in her room seems ridiculous. I mean, it's not like you need lip gloss when you're dead.

I close my eyes and breathe. Because, still, I think, way deep down, I expect to open my eyes and see her there. See Devin sitting at her vanity, brushing her hair. Or something. My eyes are closed, and then, just like the other day in the Rhodes's garden, I feel something. It's an unmistakable something or *someone*. I feel it first on my shoulder. Soft fingers holding on, and then another hand, maybe, on my other shoulder. The hair on the back of my neck rises and sways. It tickles, and I shrug to ease the feeling. Cool air rushes against my neck, then blows in soft, rhythmic whispers into my ear, again and again and again.

My heart pumps quickly. I fold my arms around myself and lift my head. "Devin?" I say again. "Devin, is that you?"

As if to answer, a feeling of hands moves up my arms and settles on my chest. Soft fingers linger over my charm; its coolness presses against me. I take in some air and bring my hand up to my charm, and for a moment it's hand on hand.

The invisible fingers move from my shoulders, tapping, touching, and slowly curl themselves around my neck. They begin to tighten, and I want to scream, but my throat constricts and nothing can get in or out. Not words. Not air. My eyes are open now, but still, there's darkness.

# BEFORE

A CAR HONKED AT US AS WE LEFT Cordeau's Jewelers and headed down the street. I'm bad with cars, but it was newish and silver and driven by two guys who were way too old for us. That didn't stop Devin.

"Come on," she said. She grabbed my hand and squeezed, yanking me toward the curb.

"What are you doing?" I asked, dragging my feet.

"What do you think?" she said, still pulling me.

"You're not going to talk to them, are you?" I asked. "Last summer you wouldn't even ride to the mall on Jared Tomassi's handlebars. Now you're going to talk to two strange guys in a car?"

Devin sighed. "A bicycle is not a hot car, and a ninth-grade boy is not a man."

We reached the car, and Devin leaned against the driver's side. The driver had pulled over a few stores down from the jewelry shop. I chewed on my fingernail. Lately things like this happened more and more.

"Were you honking at us?" Devin said, smiling sweetly. She flipped her hair over to one side and pushed the other side behind her ear.

"Would you like it if I was?" The driver was cute; I gave her that. Dark brown curls fell onto his forehead, and he had eyes the color of blueberries, with long lashes to match. He smiled, and I couldn't help

31

staring. He might have been the best-looking guy I'd ever seen in person. But he was definitely too old for her. I was totally creeped out.

"Maybe," said Devin, grinning back. She loosened her grip on my hand but didn't let go.

"I'm Greg," he said. "This is my buddy Dan." For the first time I noticed the guy in the passenger seat. He was cute, too, but he was no Greg. He was more Sears catalog while Greg was *GQ*. I totally got the sidekick gig.

"Hi," Dan said, raising his hand. His smile was more forced. He stared at us and then leaned over and whispered something to Greg that I couldn't hear.

Greg ignored him and kept talking to Devin. "It's hot out," he said. "Good thing my AC is pumped."

"Lucky." Devin nodded, still smiling. She inched closer, slowly bringing me along. "We walked all the way here, and now we have to walk back." She tilted her head. "I guess."

No, I thought to myself. No, *no*. I squeezed her hand—a signal. Don't get any closer. These guys were cute, but they were too old, much too old. Probably in college.

"Yeah, well, I can see you're hot." Greg grinned. "You know, from all that walking."

Devin tugged on my hand and pulled me toward the car. What was she *doing*?

"Are you crazy?" I whispered. I tugged back and pulled us farther away again.

Dan seemed as thrilled as I was about the situation. He leaned back into his seat and shook his head. "Come on, man, they're just kids."

Greg patted Dan on the knee. He was still smiling. "How old are you, gorgeous?" he said to Devin.

Devin sighed dramatically, teen-soap style. "What's age anyway?" She pulled on me harder, and I actually tripped forward. She shot me a can't-you-even-try-to-be-cool? look. Then she turned back to the car, put her other hand on her hip, and grinned. "Just a number."

"Actually, it's the law," said Dan, leaning forward. "Age is the law." He shook his hand in a dismissive way. "Why don't you girls go play hopscotch?"

"How rude," said Devin. "We're a bit beyond that, my friend."

"I doubt that," said Dan. "And I'm not your friend."

"Hey, hey, hey," said Greg. "Relax. No need to get all bent out of shape." He leaned on the car door and rested his elbow on the tip of the window. Thick brown hair covered his arm and curled over a silver wristwatch. "Seriously, though. You girls in high school?"

Devin moved toward the car and put her hand next to his. Her other hand still held mine. She leaned toward him. "Cass plays the guitar. Like in a band."

"Devin!" I was so not in a band, but maybe one day. Still, what was she doing?

"Really?" said Greg, totally uninterested. "A high-school band?"

"We're sophomores," I said quickly. I wanted out. I wanted to get as far away from this car as possible. All three of them turned in my direction. Devin glared at me so sharply it hurt. She dropped my hand.

33

"Crap," Greg said, rolling up the window. He didn't look at us again and peeled off down the street.

Dan, however, stuck his head out the window. He yelled at us down the street. "Didn't your mothers ever tell you not to talk to strangers?"

Devin stamped a foot and flicked him off, but I'm sure he didn't see. "Jerks!" she said. "Losers!" Ironically she looked younger than she had in a long time.

"Exactly," I said. "What were you thinking? They could've been, I don't know, dangerous."

She glared at me, then rolled her eyes.

"And telling them I'm in a band?" I said. "God, Devin."

"Oh, shut up, Cass," she said. "You wish you were."

Of course I did, and I hated that she knew that. But that wasn't the point.

"It was just for fun." She kicked at the sidewalk. "You're way too uptight. When are you going to grow up already?"

There was so much I wanted to say. So many words welled up in my throat. We were far away from the girls who'd played dress-up—who'd clomped around in Mrs. Rhodes's high heels, draped in her silk scarves. Who wanted to be fancy grown-up ladies, but only for pretend. Game over. Devin didn't get me anymore, and I didn't get her. I should have stormed away dramatically and hurled my best threats at her—that's what Devin would have done. But that wasn't me. So I did what she said. I shut up.

# AFTER

"CASS, ARE YOU UP THERE?"

It's Mrs. Rhodes. The tightness around my neck disappears, and I can breathe again. It's just Mrs. Rhodes. Just Devin's room. Just me, alone in Devin's room, right? I take deep breaths, in and out, in and out, and walk over to the large window at the far end of the room. I bring my hands up to my neck. My skin is smooth, unscarred. The charm sleeps softly against my skin. I press my forehead against the cool glass and watch as flashes of red and white headlights illuminate the street below. Just me, alone. My heart slows. *What just happened?*

"Cass?" Mrs. Rhodes is standing in Devin's doorway now. All around the doorway are the flowers Devin painted on her wall so long ago. Of course, it was always flowers for Devin.

"You're in her room," she says, still staring. Does she know? Does she realize what just happened?

I nod. "I'm sorry. I shouldn't have—"

"No, no, it's okay." She runs her long manicured fingers through her hair and sighs. "Somehow it makes me feel better, too. That's why you're up here, isn't it?"

She has no idea, does she? I nod a lot. "Yes," I say, but I don't really look at her. "I guess so."

35

Her eyes glaze over again with tears. "It's almost as if when I'm up here, she's with me." She laughs. "It's crazy, I know."

Not really, I think. Not crazy. I bring my hands up to my throat. It's sore, as though just thinking about screaming has rubbed it raw.

Mrs. Rhodes lingers in the doorway. There are no words right now; we're just staring at each other, and I wish she would move so I could get downstairs. I need to leave just as much as I needed to come up here. I need to get out of this room, out of this house. I need air. "Cass, I—are you okay?" Mrs. Rhodes rubs her eye, leaving a smudge of what's left of her mascara.

"Yes, I think—" Beneath the bed Devin's slippers have moved slightly and now face the other way, as though she'd just taken them off and slid them under there. "I'm—I'm fine." I stare at the slippers. Maybe I knocked into them by mistake? I don't remember, but . . . maybe that's what happened?

Mrs. Rhodes looks over toward the bed. "Oh," she says, her voice cracking. "Her slippers." She walks over and adjusts them, putting them back in place near the bed. She stands up and stares at me, her eyes wide and unblinking. I do the same, and for a moment, you can see the connection in the air, eye to eye, hovering between us. She thinks I moved the slippers. I know I didn't. My eyes begin to sting, and soon I blink and look away. I wonder if Mrs. Rhodes reads into that. Reads what I'm trying to hide.

If she does, she doesn't say so. "Listen, Cass, a

detective's going to call you. He wants to talk, you know, if there's anything you can tell him."

"Ah, okay." Warm beads of sweat form above my lip. I lick them off.

"I'm sorry," she says. "I know how difficult it must be for you to—to talk about things. It's just part of the process."

"I want to help. I mean, whatever I can do." I do *want* to help. But that's not everything, is it? Right now I want to leave. Right now I can't even think. *Those slippers* . . .

She nods a few times. "Yes, well, we appreciate it, Mr. Rhodes and I." She stares at me, still nodding. "We appreciate anything you can do for . . . " She clears her throat with a wet gurgling noise. "For Devin." Her voice is hoarse from tears.

She reaches toward me and gently takes my hand, just as she did the other day in her backyard. I can barely feel my hand, as though it's separate from my body, just floating there in hers. "Cass," she says, still holding on. "I hope we can talk to each other. I hope we can." She licks her lips again and pauses. "Let's help each other, okay?"

I still can't feel my hand, so it takes me a moment to realize that Mrs. Rhodes has let go. It's only my heart knocking at my chest that clues me in to the fact that I'm breathing quickly and probably too loudly. "Okay," I say, trying to slow my breath. "Okay."

"Thank you," she says.

Can she hear how loud my heart is beating? I close

my mouth and breathe through my nose, but that doesn't help. My heart can't or won't slow down.

Mrs. Rhodes straightens up and takes a deep breath. "There's a boy downstairs who says he knows you." She plays with her string of pearls.

I bite on my lip. "I saw."

"A boyfriend?" she asks, tilting her head to the side.

"Oh, no," I say. "Nothing like that." Not anymore at least.

"He seems nice," she says. "Here he is today, and he barely knew Devin, right?"

Mostly right. But they're linked. I just can't tell her that. "He's okay."

"People come out of the woodwork for these things, don't they?" I think she tries to smile, but her lips turn downward. Her mouth doesn't move that way now. Maybe it won't ever again. Mrs. Rhodes's perfect mouth, stuck forever in neutral.

"I guess so." But Marcus didn't crawl out of any woodwork. He's absolutely connected to this whole mess.

She turns away from me. "We'd better get back downstairs."

"Sure." Thank God. I follow her down the stairs. My legs shake beneath me, and I hold on to the banister to steady myself. I'm still reeling from what happened in Devin's room. What am I doing to myself? Ahead of me Mrs. Rhodes walks slowly but deliberately, also holding on to the banister. She looks old from behind.

Mr. Cordeau is at the foot of the staircase. "There

you are, Susan." He takes Mrs. Rhodes's slender hands into his large palms. "Let me tell you again how sorry I am. Truly, truly sorry."

Mrs. Rhodes looks tired, like she'd rather turn around and crawl into her bed. "Thank you, Jim," she says, looking off to the side. She slowly pulls her hands away. "We appreciate your coming by."

His gaze lingers on her, as if he's searching, but she keeps her head down. "Of course," he says. There's a hint of a frown. Susan Rhodes is grieving. Her sparkle has faded.

His eyes turn toward me. "And for you, too," he says. "Losing your best friend, and in such an . . ." He pauses. "There are simply no words."

"Thanks," I say. There are words, all right. Does he think I'll tell him those words just because he made me a best-friend charm a few weeks ago? I turn away from him. I'm allowed, given the circumstances.

"I hope you have people to talk to," he says. "When you feel the need."

My cheeks grow warm. "I do," I say. For example, Mrs. Rhodes wants to talk, even though I will never talk to her.

He turns back to Mrs. Rhodes. "Susan, dear, if there's anything I can ever do."

Mrs. Rhodes nods again, but her back is stiff and her eyes are far away. "Thank you, Jim," she says, but it's clear she's done talking. Done with all the well-meaning visitors. Mr. Cordeau pats the top of the banister, then turns quickly to me. "Well, bye, then," he says. He walks toward the front door. He looks over at Mr. Rhodes but then leaves without saying good-bye.

Mrs. Rhodes wipes tears from her eyes. "Out of the woodwork they come," she says. I look around, but Marcus is gone. My heart sinks a little, betraying my mind. It's better this way, I tell myself.

We make our way back into the living room. The *babka* I brought is now on the large table. It looks a little lost, as if it's not sure why it's there, surrounded by fish. I'd like to grab it, take it back. If the *babka* never gets eaten, maybe it will be like none of this ever happened. Maybe it will be like Devin's still alive and I'm not this person I no longer recognize.

# BEFORE

"SO, WHAT DO YOU GIRLS HAVE PLANNED for the weekend?" Devin's mother smiled at us as she chopped tomatoes. She looked like one of those chefs on the cooking channel with the checkered apron, shining silver pots, and a bottle of cooking sherry beside her. She was stealing sips from the bottle, but everything Mrs. Rhodes did was somehow elegant, even when it was happy hour at two in the afternoon.

"We'll probably go to the mall," said Devin. "Right, Cass?" She looked at me and smiled, but there was a warning behind her smile. Something hidden between her crooked grin and the flash in her eyes told me there was more. Lately there was always more with Devin. Besides I knew she was still mad about the Greg-and-Dan incident, so I was on my best behavior. I wasn't in the mood for the drama.

I nodded. "What else is there to do on the weekend when you don't have a license?"

Mrs. Rhodes laughed, which warmed me in a way I couldn't explain. She had Devin's smile but without the slight slant. Straight-up niceness.

Devin nodded at me—I had done well. I'd given the right answer, covered up whatever she had cooking, something I'm sure would have no resemblance to her mother's tilapia.

"Cass, honey," said Mrs. Rhodes, "be a love and pass me the olive oil." She licked her fingers. "It's over by the sink."

Devin was a lot closer to the sink, and I wondered why she wasn't asked. But Devin didn't seem bothered. She leafed through a fashion magazine on the kitchen table.

"Sure." I grabbed the fancy Italian-looking olive oil.

"Thanks," said Mrs. Rhodes. She grinned at me again with the perfect teeth Devin inherited. "Devin's not really much for helping in the kitchen anymore." She tilted her head in Devin's direction. "Are you, Devy?" She smiled, but there was no mistaking the edge in her voice.

Devin didn't even look up from the magazine. "Nope," she said.

Mrs. Rhodes's smile wilted. She went back to chopping tomatoes, the knife coming down on the cutting board this time with more gusto. "Do you like to cook, Cass?"

"I don't know," I said, being careful. I didn't want to be accused later of being a suck-up. "My mom doesn't cook much." Since Dad left we were all about takeout.

Mrs. Rhodes nodded. "Yes, I think I knew that." She shrugged. I silently thanked her for letting that one go. My mother would never have missed the opportunity to smear Susan Rhodes. But Susan Rhodes had class. "Come, I'll show you how to brown the fish," she says.

42

"Oh my God, Mom," said Devin. "Do you really think she cares?"

"I don't mind," I said. I offered up a little smile.

Devin shot me a look.

"Relax," I mouthed to her. Devin found her mother as annoying as I found mine, and part of me liked watching her get so worked up.

Mrs. Rhodes ignored the slight and slipped a filet into the frying pan. "Here we go," she said. "Now, Cass, you do the other one." She put her hand on my shoulder and offered me the spatula. I carefully lifted the filet off the plate.

"Good," said Mrs. Rhodes. "Careful, now, those things are slippery."

"She's just being polite," said Devin, "aren't you, Cass?" She put down the magazine and walked toward the kitchen island. "You don't really want to help, do you?"

I gripped the spatula carefully, the filet weighing it down. Mrs. Rhodes still had her hand on my shoulder, but now I felt Devin behind me, too. I felt her close, felt her breath on the back of my neck. I slid the filet off the spatula. It fell a little too quickly, and we were splattered with droplets of hot oil. I jumped back from the impact.

"Sorry!" I said.

"Nice going, spaz," said Devin.

"No worries," said Mrs. Rhodes, wiping down the counter. "It happens." She was still smiling. "The next one will be easier." She poured herself a glass of sherry.

"The next one?" said Devin. "Cass, who are you here to hang out with anyway?"

A part of me wanted to stay in the kitchen with Mrs. Rhodes and learn how to brown tilapia. It was that same part that didn't want to know what Devin really had planned for the weekend.

"Sorry," said Mrs. Rhodes. She patted me on the hand. "You girls need alone time."

I didn't want Mrs. Rhodes to feel bad. "It smells good," I said, trying to ease the tension.

Mrs. Rhodes brightened. "You're welcome to stay for dinner, Cass."

"Thanks," I said. "Maybe another night." My mother was expecting me—she hated ordering in for one.

Mrs. Rhodes leaned toward me. "What's that?" she said. She reached for the charm. "Oh," she said, tilting her head. "You got new charms?"

I nodded and sort of smiled. Didn't she know this? We'd charged them to her account.

Devin brushed right over it. "We had to. We got rid of the last ones."

"You got rid of them?" she asked.

"I don't want to talk about it, Mom."

Mrs. Rhodes nodded. "Okay." She looked at me hopefully, as if maybe I'd talk about it. But I couldn't. Of course. She brightened again, but it was clearly fake. "Well, they're lovely. Jim Cordeau's work?"

"Yes," I said, since Devin had already stuck her nose back into the magazine.

Mrs. Rhodes nodded. "I can tell. He's a wonderful designer."

Without taking her eyes off the magazine, Devin said, "He sends his love."

"He does?" said Mrs. Rhodes, lifting her head. Devin looked up to see Mrs. Rhodes flush pink. She turned back to her magazine, a satisfied smile on her face.

"I think what he said was he sends his best," I said.

Devin shrugged. "Whatever." She was now half-way out of the kitchen. "Come on, Cass," she said. "Let's go up to my room."

Mrs. Rhodes made like she was straightening up and cleared her throat a few times.

"Okay." I was about to walk out of the kitchen, when Mrs. Rhodes moved in behind me. She put her hand on my shoulder, and I turned around. "Devin's lucky to have such a good friend." Her smile seemed forced.

I nodded. "Thanks." I moved again toward the stairs, but her hand remained firmly on my shoulder.

"Your head's always been in the right place." The way she looked at me made me feel like I was supposed to open up and tell her everything she didn't know about her daughter.

Of course I couldn't do that. So I lied. It was less complicated that way. "You don't have to worry about Devin."

Mrs. Rhodes nodded and smiled, but not her usual smile. This one took work. "Mothers always worry," she said. "Choices aren't always easy." She was far away right then, so I waited for her to come back. It was the least I could do after we had fried tilapia together. She smiled again, this time a little more relaxed. "Now, off with you." She gave me a gentle nudge out of the kitchen and into the hall.

Devin was waiting on the staircase. "What was that all about?"

"Nothing," I said. "The tilapia, you know." I didn't want to start anything.

"You can stop drooling, by the way," she said. "My mother's not so perfect."

"I didn't say she was." But of course I thought it. I thought it all the time.

"At least your mom's real," she said, sighing. "What you see is what you get, like it or not."

"So is yours," I said. "They're just different." Devin leaned on the wooden stair rail and looked at me. She shook her head, then smiled. "Right, okay, Cass. Let's just go up to my room."

She headed up the staircase, then turned around. "Did you see her face when I mentioned Cordeau?" she said. "They're totally doing it."

"Devin!" My stomach twisted around itself. "There's no way. Your mother wouldn't do that. She was just embarrassed by what you said."

Devin shrugged. "Maybe. I don't care, anyway. Like I said, jewelry discounts." She skipped up a few steps.

"Still gross," I said. Besides, I didn't believe it. The Rhodeses were a great couple. Jim Cordeau was just another Susan Rhodes groupie.

Devin turned back around. "By the way, how annoying is she?" She shook her head. "What does she care if we got new charms?"

46

"She did pay for them, didn't she?" I looked at her, really looked at her, searching for the part of Devin that actually asked her mother before charging the charms to her account. Or at least her father.

Instead she scowled at me. "You wouldn't pay, remember? Your guitar—the one you *need* to buy?"

"I wouldn't have gotten the charms if your mom wasn't okay with paying for them."

"I told her about it. She forgot."

"If you say so." There was no point in arguing. No matter what I said, Devin somehow always won.

"And really," said Devin, "is it 1950? Seriously, her apron!"

I couldn't help but smile. "The sherry bottle's a nice touch, too," I added, feeling a little guilty.

Devin laughed. "Why doesn't she just use a funnel?"

I unclenched, relieved to have my friend back in my corner. And yet I thought that Devin didn't deserve to have a mother like Mrs. Rhodes. I hated that I felt this way when Devin was supposed to be my best friend. But sometimes I couldn't stop my brain from spinning out threads of bad thoughts.

# AFTER

"SOMEONE NAMED MARCUS CALLED while you were sleeping," says my mother.

I look up from my pillow, still woozy from a restless night's sleep. I can't stop thinking about what happened yesterday in Devin's room. My guitar is on the floor beside me. It's a comfort, somehow, having it there, even though I haven't played in days. "Oh," I say to her. Not ready yet to switch gears. Clearly not the response my mother hoped for.

"Well, who is he?" she asks. "A new friend? I've never heard of him before."

"Just some guy." I close my eyes. I can picture him so vividly, his face, the way his front teeth crisscross. His smile. I can picture what we almost might have had.

My mother walks into the room and runs her hands through her thick, blond supermodel hair. A remnant of her cheerleading days. "He sounded pretty bent on talking to you. Maybe you should call him back."

I realize then that Marcus probably tried calling my phone first, but it's uncharged and neglected somewhere in the house. I don't really care. I don't want to talk to anyone anyway.

My mother has other ideas. She hands me a sticky note with Marcus's name and number on it.

I don't reach for it but instead roll over onto my bed. In the once-upon-a-time before Devin died, I would have wanted nothing more than to call him back. That is, once I'd gotten over the initial shock that he'd actually called. But there are no more happy endings for me.

My mother plunks the note onto my mirror. "In case you change your mind," she says. "A little distraction would be good for you."

Distraction? Like I'll ever be able to think of anything else again?

She looks at the guitar on the floor. "Were you playing? I didn't hear."

"No."

"Why not?" she says. "Weren't you working on some songs?"

"I don't feel like playing."

"Suit yourself," she says. "But you should do something. Something besides wallowing. Write some angsty music. Get your feelings out."

I sigh—loudly, for effect. "Leave me alone."

"Well, don't leave the guitar there," she says. "Someone will trip on it."

"Not if someone stays out of my room."

My mother tries, I think, unsuccessfully, to hide her frustration. She sounds bored, as though my grief (well, it's more than grief, but she doesn't know that) should get over itself so we could go back to discussing things like her divorce, my "idiot father," my weight. Maybe I'm being unfair. It's just that I know how she felt about Devin.

"I'm just saying that you have to move on," she says. "Get out of bed. Live again." She pats my head like I'm a puppy.

When my father left, Mom had her own day in bed—but that was it. One day and then she was on spin cycle, running around as though if she stopped moving the world would stop, too.

I tune her out—a skill I've perfected—and she leaves. Now that I'm alone and fully awake, my mind takes off. I'm thinking again about being in Devin's room yesterday. About the feeling of hands, the feeling of breath on me. It was so . . . real that I wonder if Mrs. Rhodes has felt it, too. Is that what she was trying to tell me? Am I totally losing my mind? It's a dangerous thought given what I have to hide. My body grows warm. I just know what I felt and I think—no, I almost *know*—that it was Devin. Do people come back? Do they really?

And then there's the detective. A detective! How can I possibly talk to a detective? What will I say? I don't even tell my mother about that. I don't have the energy for her barrage of questions. I bury my head in my pillow.

My mother lingers in the doorway. "I wasn't trying to upset you." Again, though, I sense a prickle. We don't have too many of these mother-daughter talks. They don't usually go well.

She probably thinks I'm crying, and I let her think that. "It's okay," I say, though my voice is muffled from the pillow. I can't tell her what happened in Devin's room. The only person I can really talk to, the only one who would understand, is Mrs. Rhodes. But what if she asks too many questions?

The phone rings in the hallway. "Ooh, maybe that's him—Marcus?" my mother says, smiling. "If it is, I want you to take the call—no discussion!" The idea of a boy calling me makes her giddy. She answers the phone, and then there's silence for a while.

"Yes," she says, eventually responding. "No, it's no bother at all. I'm so sorry. I can't imagine what you're going through." Her voice is strained. "Of course, Susan, I'll let her know." Pause. "Yes, we understand," she says. "Oh, I see, of course. No, I didn't know, but—yes, yes, of course." More silence. "Oh, that's very nice of you, but I'm not sure—yes, certainly." Pause. "You take care of yourself, okay? If there's anything we can do. Right, okay. Bye." My mother's footsteps press against the Persian runner in the hallway. I'm in for it now.

I lie on my bed, my face buried in the soft down of my pillow. It's a little hard to breathe, but I don't have it in me to lift my head. Besides, there are worse things than drowning in goose feathers.

My mother's back in the doorway to my room. "A detective's coming by tomorrow?"

I nod.

She moves toward me. "Susan Rhodes told me she mentioned it to you?"

"Yeah, I think so."

"Why didn't you tell me?" she says. "It seems like something I might want to know."

I shrug. "A lot on my mind, I guess." I don't tell my mother much anyway; there's no real point. The less I say about Devin, about what happened, the better.

"Well, it was inevitable they'd start an investigation, given what happened. Young girls don't just mysteriously appear dead at the bottom of ravines. They'll be talking to everyone, as they should. Can't have a lunatic running around." My mother considers me and then shrugs again. "Unless she jumped." She sits down on the bed with a newfound sense of urgency. As if we're girlfriends dishing about an exciting date. "Do you think?"

"I—I don't know," I say, my stomach knotting up. *Don't say anything. Just don't.*

"I suppose anything's possible," she says. "Why would Devin have been out there to begin with? Doesn't make sense." She shakes her head and sighs. "Then again, Devin was wild. Who knows why she did things?" She runs her hand through her hair. "Was she drinking?"

"No!" I've startled her, and she frowns. "She wouldn't," I say. Devin didn't drink. She glared every time Mrs. Rhodes drank.

"Never say *wouldn't*," says my mother. "Kids your age experiment. And with that one—I wouldn't be surprised if—"

"Never say *wouldn't*," I say, cutting her off.

My mother pauses, then says, "Susan Rhodes

invited you over for lunch." She examines her long, polished fingernails. "Whenever you're up to it." She starts to leave the room and then adds, "Although I would think you'd talk to me before you'd talk to her."

I nod again. Somehow my mother, as always, makes it about her. "Right," I say. This isn't the first time Mrs. Rhodes has called since yesterday. I haven't called her back, and I feel bad about it. It's not that I don't want to talk; it's simply that I can't. I can't because of what I have to hide. And I can't because of what happened in Devin's room. The feeling of hands—is that what they were? The way they felt, the way they curled around my neck. The way I felt . . . something. How did Devin's slippers move? I go over it again and again. The more I think about it, the more convinced I am that it was—something. *Something.* Something not normal.

I do not want to go back to that house.

# Before

"COME ON, IT'LL BE FUN!" Devin jumped up into a sitting position on her bed. The pink patchwork quilt was still bright after all these years—a credit to Mrs. Rhodes's laundry skills.

"Why do we always have to do this?" I said. I wished we could stay in her room all day and play board games like we used to. When that was enough. Why did everything have to change? I picked a little at my guitar. The strings sounded better, but I still wanted to buy a new one.

Devin crossed her legs, the toes of her fuzzy pink slippers poking out from under her. I had the same pair in purple—we'd bought them together at the flea market—but my feet grew too fast, just like my boobs, so my own slippers were long gone.

"Live a little, Cass," said Devin. "We're just going to meet them at the mall for a few hours." "Them" was a pair of soon-to-be junior boys from another high school. Chad was a new love interest of Devin's, the other, Marcus, his wingman and my "date."

"A few hours?" I said. "I've heard that before." Devin time was like another dimension of timekeeping altogether. No formulas or anything, no relativity theories. Things lasted as long as she wanted them to, and that was that.

"What's a few hours with good company?" she said, grinning. "Smoking-hot company."

"We don't even know them," I said.

"We'll get to know them."

"How do we know they're not serial killers?" I pulled my legs under me.

"You've got to be kidding me," she said. "Jeez, they work at the WayMart. They spend their afternoons packing produce, not heat."

"So," I said, plucking at a few strings, "how do you know it's not a ploy to meet victims?"

"You're insane, Cass Kirschner," she said. "Besides, it's not a date. It's just four friends hanging out." She grinned again. "Remember that if my mother asks."

I play a few dramatic chords. *Dun-duh-duh-dun.* Devin laughs.

Okay, so I didn't really think Chad and Marcus were serial killers. But I didn't like how Devin met guys everywhere and then I had to tag along on her dates because Mrs. Rhodes wouldn't let her go by herself. I didn't like that Chad would be super cute and smooth and that halfway through the "not-a-date" he and Devin would disappear into the movie theater or behind the mall and this Marcus guy and I would probably be stranded on a hard plastic mall bench discussing bugs or baseball or whatever other annoying things this person Marcus liked.

"I don't know, Devin," I said. I stopped plucking and bit on my nail. It was soft, and a piece came off easily. "Maybe we should stop by the WayMart so I can meet him first. So I know if he's a total waste of time."

"No way," she said, shaking her head. "That'll look ridiculous. Like we don't trust Chad."

"Trust Chad?" I said. "I don't even *know* Chad." I shook my head. "And you only spoke to him for five minutes while your mom was in the next aisle buying cereal."

"Chopped meat," she said.

"What?"

"My mom was buying chopped meat, not cereal."

I sighed. "Do you always have to be right?"

"Yes," she said. "That's how I know I'm right about Chad and Marcus." Devin leaned back on her bed and propped herself up with her elbows. "I'm good at reading people."

"Really?" I said. "I can't believe you would say that after the recent Greg-and-Dan debacle."

"There was nothing wrong with them," she said.

"They were collecting Social Security benefits."

Devin rolled her eyes. "You're so off sometimes, Cass."

"Okay," I said. "What about that guy Andrew who left us at the mall when his girlfriend showed up?"

"Loser." She planted an *L* on her forehead with her thumb and forefinger.

"And that other kid, from Fairview, and his friends who tried to get us to go back to their house with them? There were like six of them and only two of us?"

"Oh, yeah," she said. "Ricky, I think. He was cute."

"He was a perv," I said.

"Your point?" She tilted her head to the side.

I sighed again. "Remember Ty, the guy from the ice-skating rink who gave you all those hickeys right before your grandma Nan came up from Florida?"

She threw her head back and laughed. "Thank God for cover-up!"

I rolled my eyes and chewed on the rubbery bit of nail in my mouth.

Devin sat up again. She looked at me, her eyes wide. "I chose you to be my best friend, didn't I?"

I stopped chewing. "That's not fair." She always threw that at me when she was trying to win an argument. Like I'm the one who was lucky. What about Devin? I stuck with her when our old group fell apart. When Lizzy and Gina decided they couldn't deal with Devin anymore. When everything blew up.

"You are not backing out, Cass. Don't do that to me." Devin's blue eyes were so piercing.

I looked down at my guitar for relief. I stretched out a few chords and pulled out some notes. I'd been working on a few of my own pieces, but right then they were all a little jumbled together.

"That sounds nice," Devin said, her voice softer.

I shrugged and played more. "Thanks."

"You're really good—you know that?"

"Sure," I said. "You just want me to go with you on Saturday."

"True," she said, leaning back. "But I wish I could do something like that. You know, like have a talent."

I raised an eyebrow. "Plenty of guys think you've got talent."

"You know what I mean."

"I guess so." I played a few more chords, and even though Devin's motives were totally transparent, I ate up the compliments. Who wouldn't? When I was finished I rested my hand on the curve of my guitar.

Devin clapped a little too dramatically, but I didn't mind. "The amazing Cass Kirschner, ladies and gentlemen," she said.

"Okay, okay," I said, grinning. "You win. I'm a sucker for applause."

"I meant every clap," she said. "Really, truly." She smiled, but there was something more to it, something sad, if that makes any sense. At that moment I actually believed her.

I gave in. "What's so great about Chad, anyway?" I said. "Mr. Supermarket Produce."

Devin flipped her hair and grinned. "I like a guy who knows what to do with melons."

"That's gross." I threw a pink patchwork pillow at her.

"Hey, and you know what?" Devin leaned forward. "I hear Marcus is especially good with cantaloupes." She poked me in the chest.

"Ow," I said. "You are so disgusting!" I hit her with another pillow.

"You mean hilarious?" She grabbed the pillow and jumped on me.

I squealed. I couldn't help it—she'd landed on my ticklish spot, and I was already laughing from the

58

produce jokes. "Stop," I said, still giggling. "I can't breathe."

Devin sat up and plopped down next to me on the bed. "Admit it, Cass," she said. "You wouldn't have any fun without me."

Maybe. Maybe that was true. "Fine," I said. "I'll go, but Marcus better not be a complete ass."

"I'm sure he will be," she said. "With a name like"—she held her nose and finished with a nasally twang—"*Marcus.*"

I threw another pillow at Devin, and she threw one at me. Soon we were rolling all over the bed again, kicking and laughing. The patchwork quilt fell to the floor in a pink heap, and it felt like the millions of times we'd done things like this before. I remembered again why she was my best friend.

We collapsed beside each other on the bed, winded from so much laughing. Devin turned toward me. She breathed in and out in short spurts, and her breath was warm and minty on my neck. I was aware of my own breath, rising and falling. I turned toward Devin and closed my eyes.

# AFTER

ENTER THE DETECTIVE. "I'm sorry," my mother says to him. "She hasn't been herself since it happened. She's usually more cooperative."

Cooperative? I'm not in preschool.

"Devin was a real handful," my mother says. "I worried sometimes that she was leading Cass down a path, if you know what I mean."

Oh, yes. My mother is revved up and ready to go.

Detective Williams sits down on the ottoman across from my new permanent spot on the couch. He's young and has honest eyes, brown like warm fudge. It's clear he really wants to help. He opens up a notepad. "Anything specific that worried you?"

"Boys," my mother says. "Risky behavior, that sort of thing." She shrugs. "You would think her parents would be more on top of her, but denial's a powerful thing." She nods knowingly—all those years of therapy have made her an expert on everyone else's lives.

"Mom!" My body bubbles with anger. She thinks somehow it's Devin's fault that this happened. Devin's fault because of who she was. The oldest argument in the book—the girl deserved it. My mother's back in the 1950s with Mrs. Rhodes's apron. She has no idea how wrong she is.

"The boy thing . . ." my mother whispers to the detective as though I'm not right there in the room with them. "Not so much of an issue with Cass."

Detective Williams looks embarrassed for me. He scribbles something in his notebook. Probably something like, *Girl dies due to boy-crazy, late-night tendencies. Not a problem for chubby friend.* If I'd eaten anything in the last day, it would be all over the couch by now.

Detective Williams sits up and stretches his long legs in front of him. "Mrs. Kirschner—"

"Gilbert," says my mother. "*Ms.* Gilbert. Cass's father and I are divorced."

"I'm sorry," he says, shifting his weight in his seat.

"I'm not," she says, grinning, and I want to climb underneath one of the couch cushions. "I already have one teenager to deal with—I didn't need another." She looks at her fingernails. "We were young—what can I say?"

I bury my head in a throw pillow. I can't stand how my mother makes her almost twenty years of marriage seem like a big mistake. Which makes me part of that big mistake.

"Ms. Gilbert," says the detective, "if you don't mind, I'd like to speak with Cassandra for a few minutes."

"Cass," I say. I'm still not talking to you, I think, but at least get my name right.

"Sorry, Cass," he says, leaning forward.

"It's fine with me," says my mother. "Honey, just tell him what you know. The sooner we figure things out, the sooner we can put it all behind us."

My ears grow warm. Put it all behind us? It will never be behind me. It will always be in front of me, staring back at me, no matter where I go. Always, always, always.

The detective clears his throat. "Can you tell me anything about what happened that evening?" he says. "Anything at all?"

I can tell you a lot, I think, but not what you want to hear. I lean into the throw pillow, so my voice is muffled. "We were at the mall that day. We go there sometimes."

"Cass," he says, "could you maybe take your face out of the pillow?"

I sigh and lift my head.

"Thanks," he says. He writes something in his notebook. "What'd you do there? At the mall?"

"We had a date."

"*Devin* had a date," my mother says, interrupting. "Cass just went along. Cass is a good girl, Detective Williams, and very musical. She plays the guitar—even writes her own songs."

"Mom." I grit my teeth.

"Interesting." The detective nods. "Yes, the two boys, we spoke with one of them, a Chad Miller." Miller? Funny, I realize then that I never knew his last name. Did Devin?

Detective Williams wonders the same thing. "How well did Devin know Chad Miller?" he asks.

I shrug.

"Mr. Miller told me he met Devin when he was working produce at the WayMart."

62

He leans forward. "Is that your understanding?"

Mr. Miller? Suddenly Produce Chad the überjock sounds like a high-school principal. "I guess so," I say. "I mean, that's what she told me."

"He's not from your school?" asks the detective.

I shake my head.

"He's a little older? A junior, I believe. Does that sound right?"

"A junior?" says my mother. "There aren't enough boys your own age?"

"It's just one year, mom," I say.

Detective Williams ignores our side conversation. "What did you think of Chad Miller," he says, "when you first met him?"

Chad Miller. Chad Miller. My head hurts. Why do I have to think about Chad Miller at all? "Typical dumb jock." I shrug. "I didn't really talk to him." He didn't really talk to me.

Detective Williams writes that down, too, I guess. "Thanks." He nods. "Anything else?"

I roll back over onto the couch. "No."

Detective Williams looks at me for a moment, then nods. "Okay," he says. "Now, Cass, wasn't one of the boys with you?"

"It was a friendly thing," says my mother. "My daughter doesn't date."

"Please, Ms. Gilbert," he says. He's losing patience with my mother, but he's too polite to show it. "I'd like to hear from Cass."

My mother frowns and steps away from the couch. "Sorry," she says, clearly irritated.

"Devin was with Chad; I hung out with Marcus," I mumble. All true.

"Did you?" says my mother, raising an eyebrow.

Detective Williams leans forward again. "So, you didn't know that, Ms. Gilbert?"

She shrugs dramatically. "Not the details. You know how teenage girls can be. So secretive."

I seriously, seriously need to vomit. Only my mother could turn an interrogation into a gossip session.

"So *that's* why he's calling," she says, raising her eyebrows.

"Marcus Figueroa called you?" asks Detective Williams. "Since the night of the, uh, incident?"

"Yes," I say. Even now I like the sound of his name—the cadence of it. *Marcus Figueroa, Marcus Figueroa, Marcus Figueroa.*

The detective leans forward. "What did he want? Did he say anything?"

"She wouldn't take his call. Bad date, maybe," says my mother. "Although he seems like a nice kid. Polite, friendly."

"I don't want to talk about it," I say. I wish there were someone I could tell about our night together. I never had the chance, never had the chance to gossip, moon, revel, anything like a normal teenager. It all happened so quickly, and then Devin was dead.

"Okay," says the detective. "We'll come back to that." He writes some more in his notebook. "Cass, walk me through what happened next."

"We saw a movie."

"Which movie?"

64

Which movie? What did Devin and Chad see when they left us in the mall? Some stupid car movie? "*Burning Rubber*?" I say, realizing too late that my answer sounded more like a question.

Detective Williams doesn't comment but writes something down in his notepad. "Do you still have the ticket stub?"

"No," I say. "Why would I? You can't reuse them."

He shrugs. "Sometimes people save those, you know, as mementos."

"Right," I say. Like I need a memento to never forget that day. That, and the fact that I never had a ticket stub to *Burning Rubber*. I'm not a total liar—Marcus and I considered seeing it before we ended up where we ended up. Here's the thing: if we had gone, if we had seen that stupid car movie, things would've been totally, absolutely different.

"What next?" says Detective Williams.

"We went home."

"You went home?" He rubs his chin and sighs. "Cassandra—sorry, Cass, you and I both know Devin never made it home that night."

I don't answer. I roll over on the couch and bury my face in the throw pillow again. My brain is pounding at the inside of my skull. It wants out. It wants me to lose it. And given everything that's happening, I just might oblige.

"Look," says the detective, "I know this isn't easy, but you want to help your friend, don't you?"

Help my friend? I sit straight up, and the words come out fast and harsh. "It's a little late for that, isn't it?" My stomach turns on itself and pushes something upward, something soft and salty, like sour oatmeal.

Detective Williams nods. He is really young, and I feel bad. He's trying to do his job, but I can't help him. Not in the way he wants. I can't. I wish I could, but I just can't.

Detective Williams shakes his head. "We can still find out what happened. We can still find out if someone's responsible."

"Please, Cass," says my mother. "Just tell us what you remember."

They both look at me. Detective Williams has been patient, but I sense his restlessness growing. My mother is exasperated. She even looks at her watch.

How easy would it be for me to tell them what I know? The things I said that night? The things I did? How easy would it be to let the words uncurl from around my tongue and glide slowly into the space between us? Let them light up the room in bright-orange neon: Here's your answer! Here's what you need to know! It's an incredible feeling to have that kind of power. To know that your words could change everything.

# Before

"IT'S ME," SAID DEVIN when I answered my phone.

"I know." I liked how she said "It's me," as though anyone else ever called me. I liked that even though she was most of the reason no one else called, Devin made me feel like I was someone whose phone rang all the time.

"So, it's all set," she said. "We're meeting Chad and Marcus Saturday night at the mall. After dinner, okay?"

I gnawed on my fingernail. "Do we have to?"

"Seriously, Cass?" Devin said. "I'm getting tired of this."

That stung. "We haven't gone to a movie, the two of us, in a long time." I knew Devin didn't care about things like that anymore. It's just that I wished she did.

"What do you mean?" she said. "We saw *True Night* a few weeks ago."

"Not really," I said. "You left halfway through when that kid Corey from your science class showed up."

"So?" she said. "You got to eat the rest of the popcorn. How bad could it have been?"

My hand went instinctively to my stomach. "Hilarious," I said.

She laughed. "Next time I promise we'll go together," she said. "But this time is about Chad, because I promised him."

"You promised Chad?"

"Sure," she said. "And a promise is a promise."

"To Chad?"

Her voice iced over in that way that it had been lately. "Don't do this, Cass. You'd better not do this. I swear to God, Cass . . ." She stopped. All I heard was her breath on the other end of the phone. As she breathed I held my own breath.

"Please, Cass," she finally said, her voice warming. "Okay?"

I exhaled. Devin had made up her mind, and in the end I always went along. "Fine," I said. Maybe this time it would be different. Maybe. "But you owe me a movie."

"You're the best, Cass-girl, the best. I really mean it."

Even though I'm pretty sure she didn't mean it, I still held on to her words because she had given them to me and so they were mine.

"My dad'll drive," Devin said.

"Okay," I said, trying but failing to get my voice up to that excited, sparkly octave.

"It'll be fun," she said. "I promise. That's my promise to you."

"Sure," I said. Devin's promises weren't worth much these days, unless of course, you were Chad.

"Okay, gotta run," Devin said. "Mom's taking me shopping. Gotta find something cute to wear."

"Have fun," I said, even though shopping with my mom was the exact polar opposite of fun.

"I will," she said, confident, like a person who actually found cute clothing that fit. "You might want to find something to wear, too."

An arrow to the gut. "Yeah, I know." I pulled on the waistband of my cargo pants, the only pants I owned that didn't create a giant muffin top.

"Talk to you later," she said, and hung up.

I flopped down onto my bed. Fate sealed for another Saturday night. My mother knocked on my door, and I knew she'd been listening.

"What?" I said. I picked up my guitar and played a few chords.

She pushed open the door. "Something you're working on?" she said.

"I guess so." That wasn't why she was there, of course. She'd never been that into the guitar thing—especially since my dad was the one who got it for me.

"Where are you and Devin going this weekend?"

"The mall," I said, striking another chord. "Where do we ever go?"

Her face puckered. "Alone?"

I knew that she knew what we were doing because she'd been eavesdropping. But I was annoyed, so I made her pull it out of me slowly.

"No," I said. "Devin's dad is taking us."

She leaned against the door. "I assume he's not staying."

"Of course not," I said. I kept playing. "That would be pretty loserish, don't you think?"

"Interesting word," she said, shaking her head. She moved farther into my room. "And the boys you're meeting? Are they staying?"

"You guessed it, Mom," I said. "There are boys." I shrugged and rested my hand on the guitar. "But it's not a date."

"I know," she said. "That's the party line." She sat down on my bed. She didn't look at me but instead reached for Pinky, my one-eyed stuffed koala. She smoothed his worn fur with her hand. "I wonder if perky Susan Rhodes knows that her daughter runs around with so many boys. Then again, it's not surprising."

"What's that supposed to mean?" I said. I strummed lightly, just a little melody without a chorus. My mother couldn't stand that Mr. and Mrs. Rhodes were happily married. She took their lack of misery personally.

"You live in a community, you hear things."

What was my mother trying to say? Mrs. Rhodes was a model mom. All PTA-ish and Girl Scout-y.

"You don't talk to anyone," I said.

She frowned at the dig. "Never mind. I spoke out of turn."

I wanted to know what she meant, what she was really saying about Susan Rhodes, but I didn't want to give her the satisfaction of asking.

"All I know," she added, "is that *you* wouldn't act like that."

It made me mad that it didn't even occur to my mother that I might, as she put it, "run around" with a boy. She saw my fat as some sort of modern-day Great Wall that no boy warrior, no matter how horny or sex-crazed, would ever scale.

"It's one guy and his friend," I said. Then I lied: "They seem nice."

"You met them?" she asked.

"Sure," I lied again.

"Would you put that thing down for a minute?"

I obliged and placed the guitar beside me.

My mother sighed. She didn't believe me. "It's not that I have a problem with you dating," she said. "I mean you're fifteen for goodness' sake. When I was your age . . ." She laughed softly, then shook her head. "It doesn't matter. Your father put an end to all that."

"So there's no problem," I said, which was ridiculous given how I felt about going. But I couldn't stand when she took digs at Dad. Even though, well, he'd left me, too.

"You don't have to go," my mother said. "In fact, I'd rather you didn't."

I rolled my eyes. "I know and I know." I kind of wished I could say to Devin, "Sorry, but my mom found out we're meeting two strange boys at the mall and she said I can't go." But Devin would never have accepted that and then, well, I didn't want to go to that place in my head, that place where I said it, and she got angry, and I was left alone. I didn't want to be the next Gina or Lizzy. And at least they still had each other.

My mother sat up straighter but still kneaded

Pinky between her fingers. "Why don't you go to the mall with Gina and Lizzy, instead? I'll bet they know nice boys."

I raised my eyebrows. "We're not even speaking to them."

"I'm sure that's not *your* fault."

I wondered sometimes if Gina and Lizzy would forgive me. I didn't think so. I hadn't fought for our friendship—just stood there mute as Devin tore it apart. "It's only a movie, Mom," I said. I picked the guitar up and started to play again, louder this time.

"Do what you want." She tossed Pinky onto the bed. Then she got up and headed toward my door. Just before she left she turned back to me. She stared at me, and my stomach twisted around itself.

"Aren't you tired, Cass?" she said. "Aren't you tired of playing second fiddle to Devin? Of always being her shadow? Aren't you just done with all of this?"

"It's not that way, Mom," I said. But it was. It so very much was. And I hated my mother for putting it out there. Her words hovered in the vast space between us. I stared back at her, into her green eyes like mine. "Just go," I said

She shook her head but didn't say a word. Then she left my room, shutting the door behind her.

I picked up my guitar again and played and played until my fingers ached and the light from outside my window all but disappeared.

# AFTER

MY MOTHER BRINGS OUT a fresh pot of coffee. "Would you like some?" she asks Detective Williams.

"No, thank you, ma'am," he says. "Had my fill this morning at the station."

She looks annoyed. My mother's not used to people refusing things from her. "I'll pour you a cup anyway," she says. "In case you change your mind."

The detective smiles, clearly a little uncomfortable, and accepts the steaming cup. He takes a polite sip, then places the coffee on a waiting coaster. My mother smiles—the detective has good manners. She'd flirt with him if he were any older. Lucky for us all, he's not.

"Let's keep going," he says, leaning forward. He stares at me with his large brown eyes. "When was the last time you saw Devin?"

"At the mall," I say. I sit up and hug the throw pillow close to my body.

Detective Williams writes again in his notebook. "That seems to be what everyone says." He sighs and shakes his head.

"Well," says my mother, "whoever helped her into the ravine isn't going to admit it."

I look up at her. Her arms are folded across her chest, as though she thinks this is all a waste of time.

73

She thinks Detective Williams is way off the trail, ice cold. Arctic cold. She's wrong.

Detective Williams raises his eyebrows but keeps his cool. "Thank you, Ms. Gilbert," he says. "We've considered that."

She shrugs and takes a sip of coffee.

"So you play the guitar?" he says to me.

"A little," I say.

"What do you mean 'a little'?" says my mother. "You play all the time." She turns to the detective. "It's like an appendage."

I glare at her. "I don't feel much like playing anymore."

"Of course." The detective nods. "Was that something you did with Devin? Something that reminds you of her?"

"I guess," I say, but that's not what it is. The last time I played wasn't for Devin.

"I understand." Detective Williams nods. "Must be painful."

I shrug.

He leans forward. "That's a nice necklace you're wearing."

Without thinking I bring my hand up to my neck and cover the charm. "Um, thanks."

"Who has the other half?" he says.

"What?" I say.

"My kid sister has one of those. You get half; your best girlfriend gets the other. Am I right?" He's smiling, and his teeth are beyond white. Of course he's right. And he knows it.

I bite my lip.

"I guess Devin had the other half?"

"Yes," I say, looking away. I play with a loose thread on the throw pillow.

"Where'd you get it?" he says.

By the look on her face, my mother's wondering the same thing. She knows I wouldn't dip into my guitar fund. "Devin's parents paid for it."

Her eyes grow wide. "You let them? We are not a charity case, Cass."

"We charged it to their store account," I say, looking back down. "I'll pay them back."

"Which store account?" says Detective Williams.

"Cordeau Jewelers." Instinctively I reach for the charm and twirl it around, between my fingers.

My mother's face relaxes. In the end I think she doesn't care where it came from as long as she didn't spring for it.

"Right, the place in town," he says. He writes something in his notebook. "Do you know if she was wearing it the night she died?"

I nod. "She was." I roll over onto the throw pillow. "She always wore it."

"We haven't found it," he says. "We've been looking," he says, leaning back onto the couch. "Devin's mother, Mrs. Rhodes, told us about it, told us she would've been wearing it. Told us it was important to Devin, that it meant a lot."

It did. It meant everything. There could be only one reason why it was missing. "I don't know why," I say. "Maybe it fell off?" Please don't ask anymore, please.

He nods. "Maybe. But then I think we might've found it nearby."

I grip the throw pillow more tightly.

Detective Williams nods. He leans forward again and clasps his hands together. "Would Devin have taken it off herself?"

I shrug. "I don't think so—I mean, I don't know." *Please, please stop asking.* "You're not supposed to take them off."

The detective nods. "You two have a fight?"

"A fight? I—"

"A squabble, disagreement? I know how teenage girls can be. Like I said, I have a kid sister. She's always getting into it with her friends. A lot of drama." He turns to my mother. "Teenage girls, right, Ms. Gilbert?"

My mother purses her lips. "One-sided, maybe. Cass is very level-headed. Thankfully she takes after me."

"Aw, come on, Ms. Gilbert," says the detective. He picks up the cup of coffee, but then puts it down again without taking a sip. "There're two sides to every story. Especially when boys are involved."

I squeeze the pillow against my chest. I don't like how he's painting us, painting Devin and me into some melodramatic teen-girl stereotype. We weren't like that.

"Look," he says. "Right now we don't know how Devin ended up in Woodacre Ravine. But we do know that sometimes when people are emotional, they do things they wouldn't normally do." He leans forward. "Do you understand, Cass?"

"I guess." My heart definitely understands. It's starting to pound at my chest because it knows—*I know*—that Detective Williams is closer than he probably thinks.

"Where'd you last see her, Cass?" he asks. "You can tell me. I just want to make everything right. I know you do, too."

"I told you, at the mall. I . . ." Air rushes through me and out of me. My breath speeds up, and blood pulses in my ears—the sound is deafening. My heart keeps going faster. I lean over and cover my ears, but I can't stop the sound. I can't.

My mother moves closer. "Cass?" She touches my head, but I push her away. She stares at me. "What's wrong, Cass?"

Detective Williams moves forward. "Are you okay?" he says. "What's going on? Is she okay?"

The sounds pass through me, around me. Sounds everywhere, like wind, like air. It's *her*. She's with me. Moving *through* me. Devin's here—I feel her everywhere, the chill of her presence. I'm not in her house, but still, somehow, she's *here*. Her breath on my neck, just like the other day in her room. Her fingers run through my hair, down my arm. The world and its sounds fade, and I can barely hear anything else. I breathe in and out, in and out, my heart pushing at me.

"Do you hear that?" I look up at my mother, at the detective.

"Hear what, Cass?" says my mother. "What's going on?"

Again Devin's fingers—I know they're hers—curl

around my hand and squeeze until I hear the crunch of bone on bone. Over and over. Why can't they hear her? Why are they staring at me like that?

Her hands, her fingers, move toward my neck. They graze my chain, lingering over it. The air around me freezes.

The hands, *her* hands, grab onto my chain.

I scramble backward on the couch. I cover my ears and press down hard. She's angry with me. How could she not be? Wherever Devin is, *whatever* she is now, she's angry with *me*. At me, at me, at me. I curl into the throw pillow and scream.

# BEFORE

"I JUST NEED TO RUN IN AND OUT," Devin said as we neared Dreyer's Pharmacy and Surgical Supplies. "You don't have to come in if you don't want to."

We were on a cosmetics run. Well, Devin was. She was almost out of her trademark brown lip gloss and wanted to restock before the date. "I don't mind," I said. I didn't have anything else to do anyway.

She squeezed me quickly. "You're the best."

"Clearly," I said.

We walked together into the store.

Devin turned to me. "I know you have an aversion to makeup," she said, "so you can wait here if you want."

"I don't have an aversion to makeup," I said. "God, you sound like my mother."

"Well, she's not all bad, then, I guess."

"Ha, ha," I said. "I don't like the way makeup feels." It always felt sticky and oily, like I was wearing a mask. It just wasn't me.

Devin rolled her eyes. "It's not about the way it feels, Cass; it's about the way it looks. You'll have to get used to it at some point." She shrugged. "Besides, it's all about having the right moisturizer."

"I doubt that," I said.

"Look," she said. "I'll be right back. Wait here for me, okay?"

"Okaaay." I was eyeing the candy counter anyway. As soon as Devin disappeared down an aisle, I quickly bought myself a caramel nut bar, then headed back to the front of the store to eat it. I wasn't supposed to be eating candy these days, so I jumped at the opportunity to do it on the sly.

An old woman, her gray hair all fly-away, reached in front of me for a Dreyer's circular. "Excuse me, honey," she said. I moved backward, and she smiled.

She stayed there, just to the left of me, examining each page as though it were a bestseller.

I stood there, people watching, eating the candy bar as quickly as I could so I wouldn't have to hear Devin's comments about it when she came back. It slid down easily, in chunks of sweet, salty chocolate.

"You call this a sale?" said the old woman, looking up from her circular. She clucked her tongue. "Not at these prices."

I couldn't imagine ever being so old that drugstore sale circulars were actually interesting. Then again there was something oddly comforting about having nothing else to worry about but clipping coupons.

I smiled at her and shrugged, then licked a stray piece of nut from my lip. I was almost done with the chocolate bar when I saw Devin walking quickly toward me. I shoved the rest of the chocolate bar into my pocket.

Devin hurried over, her hand deep inside her own pocket. She grabbed me.

"Come on," she said.

"Don't you need to pay?" I asked.

The old woman looked up from the circular and raised an eyebrow.

"They didn't have the right color," she said. "I'll have to try another store."

The old woman frowned and went back to her circular.

"Really?" I said. "How many people wear that color? It's kind of—"

Devin giggled in a weird, un-Devin-like way. "Let's go, Cass, okay? I told my mom I'd be home by five o'clock, and we're cutting it close."

"Fine with me," I said.

The old woman nodded. "Good girl, listening to her mother." She hobbled off, circular in hand.

We headed out the store and onto the sidewalk. Devin looped her arm through mine and pulled me down the street.

"What's the rush?" I said, choking down the hunk of chocolate still in my mouth.

Devin didn't say a word but kept tugging at me. I almost tripped on a crumbling piece of sidewalk.

"Slow down," I said.

She didn't stop until we reached the corner and turned down the next street. Finally she let go of my arm. "Here," she said, slightly out of breath. She looked around quickly, then pulled her other hand out of her pocket and produced a stick of brown lip gloss.

"But you said—"

"Yeah, I know," she said. Her cheeks flushed red. "But that old hag with the circular was staring me down. I wasn't about to tell her I stole it."

"You stole it?" I said. "Are you crazy?"

"Crazy? No," she said. "The owner of free lip gloss? Yes." She opened the top and put some on her lips. She smacked her lips together and smiled. "Looks fabulous, no?"

"You shouldn't have done that," I said. "I mean, stealing? God, Devin." I shook my head. "If you needed money, I would've lent it to you."

She pouted. "What, dig into your guitar fund?"

"Yes," I said. "If it meant you wouldn't shoplift."

Devin shrugged. "I can get money from my father. This is just more fun." She winked at me. "Don't you think?"

"Uh, *no*." I said. "Not fun at all. Don't do it again, okay?"

Devin saluted me. "Aye, aye."

"It's not funny."

"It is a little," she said. She held up her thumb and forefinger and pressed them to about an inch apart. "Maybe this much?" She was still smiling, and it was clear that she was proud of herself. She was actually proud that she stole that lip gloss. She didn't care one bit that she had broken the law.

"What if you'd gotten caught?" I said.

"With this?" she said, holding up the gloss. "It's so small. Do you honestly think one of those sales clerks would report me? What do they make, like five dollars an hour? It's not worth the trouble."

The chocolate aftertaste in my mouth grew sour. "Just return it, Devin. Tell them it was a mistake—you forgot to pay. No harm done." I reached into the pocket of my cargo pants and pulled out a few dollar bills. "Seriously I'll lend you the money."

Devin's eyes narrowed. "Are you kidding?" She backed up. "I got away with it."

I dug my hands back into my pockets. The rest of my chocolate bar lay hidden inside, safe. It was a comforting thought, more classic fat-girl behavior, but still. I ran my hands along the smooth wrapper. "Well, if I were you, I would. I mean honesty's the best policy, right?"

"Really?" she said, raising an eyebrow. "Look at you, playing all innocent, Cass Kirschner," she said. "As if you didn't just secretly scarf down a chocolate bar."

"I . . ." My cheeks grew warm, and I stopped myself from saying anything else. I squeezed what was left of the candy bar between my fingers. Warm, soft chocolate oozed out onto the lining of my pocket.

# AFTER

"I'M TELLING YOU SOMETHING'S WRONG with her," my mother says. She's speaking in a low voice down the hallway from my room, but my mother couldn't whisper for all the free cosmetics on earth. "She won't leave her room unless I force her, and she's acting, well, bizarre. She won't even play her guitar, and you know, I usually have to pry that thing away from her."

It doesn't take a nuclear physicist to figure out that she's speaking to my father. They don't talk much—a few phone calls here and there to discuss child support and plane tickets. So I'm actually surprised that he's on the other end of the phone since I'm not visiting anytime soon.

"Well, of course she has a right to be upset. The whole thing is incredibly disturbing. Yes." She's quiet for a moment, obviously listening to my dad. "No, no idea at all."

"To be frank," she says, "a little crazy. She had, I don't know, a meltdown. When the detective was here. Really, Jonathan," she says. "A meltdown."

Is that what it looked like? Let her think that, I guess. Better that my mother think I had a meltdown than she know the truth. The insane truth? That some part of Devin is still actually here, that she's haunting me. And the more I think that, the more I think maybe I am crazy. Oh, my God, I wish I were crazy. Crazy would at least make sense.

"Well, maybe *you* want to talk to her," my mother says. "She doesn't listen to me—you know that," she says, her voice rising.

I roll over again on my bed. I'm not getting on the phone with my father. We were close once—we played guitar together, duets and stuff. Before he hopped a plane and landed three states away in a condo complex filled with single parents, retirees, and too much potted greenery. Before he decided he needed to "find himself," which is so clichéd, it's embarrassing. I don't hate him, but that conversation, the one my mom is suggesting, isn't going to happen.

"I'm trying to get her out of the house. She's getting weird, moping around all day."

Yeah, Mom. Thanks for your support.

"No," she continues. "She won't leave the house. Stubborn as her father," she says, getting in her digs where she can. "Well, of course it's more than that," she adds, sighing. "Obviously."

There's a long pause. I scratch an itch on my forehead, then stretch my legs. My back is starting to hurt but not enough to motivate me off my bed. In a strange, twisted way, I'm kind of glad that my parents are actually talking. This might be the longest conversation they've had in, like, eons.

"Fine," she says. "You can talk to her. . . . No, really," she says. "I'm putting you on the phone with her, Jonathan. It won't kill you to parent once in a while, or do you have a golf game?" There's another pause. "Well, there are things I resent, too," she says.

My parents can't *not* fight, and it's a relief for me to hear them. I'm comforted by the familiar rhythm of their bickering. It reminds me of a time not that long ago, when it actually bothered me. When their fighting and the too many folds of flesh on my body were worth being upset about. When my world made sense, even if I didn't like it that much.

I hear my mother's footsteps coming down the hallway. She's still in her heels from work, so her clomps are extra loud.

"She's involved with boys now," she says.

I turn my lip around between my teeth. She sounds so teen therapist when she says it. So "How does this make you feel?" So "Let's try to figure out what this means."

"I don't know," she says. "The boy called the house." She pauses. "No, she won't talk to him. She was out with him the night it all happened, and I think she's traumatized. Bad timing, I guess." Another pause. "I don't appreciate that. I didn't have trouble with boys at her age. You, of all people, should know that."

Gross, too much information. Even in my current, messed-up state I realize that.

More silence from my mom. "Maybe you should talk to her," she finally says. "I'm putting your daughter on the phone." She's right at my bedroom door. "What?" she says. "Now wait a minute." Her footsteps disappear again down the hallway.

I'm not getting on the phone with him anyway. In all fairness to my father, even if he were here, even if he'd never left us, this is not something we can talk about. Not something that he or anyone else would ever understand. What could I possibly say? *My best friend is haunting me.* What could he possibly say? *You deserve to be haunted, but it's tee time, so I'll catch you later.* I roll onto my pillow and shut my eyes.

*CLUNK!* I scramble to a sitting position and scan the room. Nothing. What was that? I hear it again. *CLUNK!* The noise is against my window. *CLUNK!* *CLUNK!* It's coming from outside. Devin? My heart hurls itself against my chest. She's back again. She's outside. She's . . . I jump up and run over to the window. Our front lights are out, but, from the light of the street lamp across the street, I can see his shape. My heart slows. Marcus is in the overgrown rhododendron bushes, tossing rocks at my bedroom window. My body unclenches. I press my face against the glass, and he waves.

He's looking up at me, almost not blinking, and even with very little light, I lose myself for a moment and marvel at how good-looking he is and at the fact that he's standing outside my window. *My* window. What crazy, misguided forces of nature had their hand in *this* little bit of fortune? In another time this would be so Romeo and Juliet. He motions again. He wants me to open the window.

My heart is beating faster now. I shouldn't talk to him. God, there are so many reasons why I shouldn't—

I know that. But, oh, I want to. My mother is down the hallway. What if she hears us? I shake my head and mouth, "I can't."

Marcus moves closer to the house. "Come on," he mouths. "Please."

I take a deep breath. We are so not Romeo and Juliet, and I so don't deserve the tragic romance of this scenario—but I unlock my bedroom window and pull it open. I lean against the cool screen.

"Hey," he says. He tries to whisper, but I'm high above him in my window—my Capulet balcony—so his voice carries.

"Hey."

"Sorry about the rocks," he says, shrugging. "I tried to use small ones."

"It's okay," I say. "We already have holes in the screen." I stick my finger through one of them and wiggle it around.

Marcus smiles, and I melt from the normalcy of it all. I wish it were a few weeks ago—I'd have given anything for this back then.

"So, uh, how are you?"

I shrug. "You know."

He nods a couple of times. "Sure, okay. I can't even—I mean—it's gotta be hard."

"Yeah."

"At Devin's house, you looked, I don't know"— he licks his lips—"different."

I am different. Marcus sees it because he sees *me*. No one can be the same after what I did. Every last molecule rearranged. "It was cool of you to go," I say.

"Not really." He looks at me and shrugs. "I had an ulterior motive."

My heart makes a sudden motion. "Oh." Dumb, I don't even know what to say.

Marcus stuffs his hands into his pockets. "I called a few times."

This time I nod. "I know. I'm"—I push some hair behind my ear—"I'm sorry. I haven't been, you know."

"Yeah, I figured." He looks up at me, then down again at his feet.

My mother's still arguing with my father. I keep an ear on the door—that could go on indefinitely or end in an abrupt hang-up. There's no way of knowing. I am poised for the dash back to my bed.

Marcus looks around, then back up at me. "Cass, I need to talk to you."

My stomach's all in a tangle. There's nothing more to say; we can't go back. It's done. "Why?" I say, even though I know the answer.

"Because, I think, well"—he nods again—"we need to talk about what happened." His eyes flicker. "Cass, there's a detective. He came to see me."

Of course he did. Detective Williams isn't playing around. He'll get to all of us. "I know. Me, too." And I also know that he'll be back. He'd been freaked out by what had happened to me that afternoon—who wouldn't have been? But he also wasn't buying the grieving-friend routine.

Marcus nods as if he's thinking things over. "I told him, I mean, I told him everything I could. There's only so much—you know what I mean?"

I haven't eaten, but something sour is pushing its way up from my stomach. I guess now Detective Williams knows more than I wanted him to. "We can't change what happened."

"Yeah, but—" He looks around. Then he looks up again at me. "Can you come down?"

I want to come down but not to talk. I want to run to him, curl into him, and let myself go. It's beyond tempting. I shake my head again. "My mom's right down the hall. She's talking to my dad."

"How's that going?" he asks.

"How do you think?"

He nods sympathetically—he gets that. He gets *me*. God, my heart literally hurts.

"Tomorrow?" he says. "Maybe somewhere else a little less"—he tilts his head—"complicated?" There's hope in his voice. *Hope*. I almost remember that feeling.

I breathe in again. "I don't think so."

My mother's heels clomp back down the hallway. "Hold on," she says. "I'm putting you on with her right now."

"I gotta go," I say.

"Cass, wait."

I let my hand linger on the screen for just the smallest of moments. Then I turn away and jump back into my bed, my heart racing from the effort.

My mother walks in, but I'm ready for her. I lie silent and still. I hold my breath.

She moves into the room until I feel her leaning over me, watching me. The scent of her perfume hangs in the air, and her breath is warm on my face. I'm reminded of when I was little and would pretend to be asleep because it was past my bedtime and I didn't want to lose dessert the next night. She reaches down and touches me just slightly on the shoulder.

But I don't move. I'm that good.

# BEFORE

"So, do you like it?" Devin twirled around in her room, supermodel style, holding the shirt up to her chest.

"Did you steal that, too?" I asked.

She shot me a look. "No. I bought it with my mom."

"It's nice, I guess." Devin was small, but the shirt looked like it would fit a first-grader. Like it should have a glittery rainbow on it.

"That's it?" she said. "It wasn't cheap."

"It should've been," I said. "How much fabric is there anyway?"

She laughed. "It's supposed to be fitted, as if you didn't know that."

I smiled back despite the fact that I'd never be able to wear that kind of a shirt, except as maybe a headband. "You're not really going to wear that, are you?"

Devin rolled her eyes at me. "Of course I am," she said. "It's summer. Light and breezy, I say."

"You sound like a tampon commercial."

She frowned. "You sound like you need a tampon." She turned away from me and faced the long mirror hanging inside her closet door. "I had to beg a little for this shirt. Mom finally gave in but yammered on again about how I should still be babysitting."

"You did pretty well in your heyday," I said. "You were good at it."

92

"I was, wasn't I?" she said, almost thoughtfully. "Who has time for that anymore?" she frowned. "It's fine when you're a kid with nothing else to do on the weekend. I've got better things going on now than wiping butts and noses and reading bunny books at bedtime."

"Like shoplifting?"

Devin scowled. "Let it go, Cass," she said. "You're getting really annoying with that."

"Just saying." I shrugged. "Babysitting's not so bad."

"Oh, yeah, I forgot you still do that. The McKenna kid, right?"

"He's sweet. It's fun, actually."

She shook her head. "You would think that."

I blinked a few times. "Since when is earning money not cool?" When I finally hold that new guitar, I'll have earned it—it'll be all mine. When we were younger, Devin and I used to pool babysitting funds. We'd buy candy, bracelets, lip gloss. These days, though, I never told her what I had in the bank. If I did, I'd be paying for everything.

She changed the subject back to her. "Okay, you made it clear you don't like my outfit," she said, folding up the shirt and placing it back inside her dresser drawer. "What are you wearing Saturday night?"

I shrugged again. "I don't know."

"Cass, are you kidding? We have a date in three days."

"I thought it wasn't a date."

She frowned. "You know it is."

"Fine," I said, "but it's your date. I'll be lucky if I

don't die of boredom listening to Marcus Button-Down, the Wing-Tipped Wonder."

"You are so negative, Cass. Just because your mother hates men doesn't mean you should."

"I don't hate men," I said. "And neither does my mother." She really didn't, actually. She just hated my father.

"Whatever." Devin shook her head, then brightened. "I can come shopping with you," she said. Her voice floated up an octave to that happy place where the skinny girls lived. "It would be fun. We haven't done that in forever. It'll be like old times. Remember how we used to try on all those clothes at the same time and totally piss off the salespeople?"

"Right," I said. "All the saleswomen at Lola's practically had wanted posters of us in the dressing rooms."

"All those white sweaters at once," she said. She waddled from side to side. "Stay-Puffed Marshmallow Girls!"

She gave me a fist bump. We laughed together again, and for a moment I was lighter. Shopping with Devin was a blast before she was this Devin. We'd buy matching T-shirts or sweaters, and I didn't care that we weren't the same size and that my shirt or sweater bulged where hers lay flat. That was all before Devin had something to say about everything I wore. She wasn't the old Devin anymore, and we couldn't wear matching clothes, and I would never, ever go clothes shopping with her again.

"Thanks," I said, "but I'm going with my mom later

this week." Ginormous lie. I hated shopping with my mother just as much as I hated shopping with Devin. I was all about closet shopping. It's what I always did. It was amazing what I could find buried at the bottom of mine, when I looked hard enough.

"Really?" she said, raising an eyebrow.

"Yes, *really.*"

"Just don't wear those." Her eyes found their way to my cargo pants, with the natty drawstring and crease lines in the thighs.

"I wasn't planning to," I said. Though of course I was.

"Sure you weren't," she said, smiling. She walked toward me, then sat down beside me on the bed. She took a few strands of my hair into her hands and ran her fingers through them. It was sweet almost, like when we were younger and would braid each other's hair. I was warm all over, and my muscles un-clenched.

"Listen, Cass," she said, leaning in. She let go of my hair, and it fell back onto my shoulder. "Do your-self a huge favor. Put on a little lip gloss and get something to wear that doesn't have drawstrings and pockets. Play up the guitar thing. Some guys like rocker chicks." She paused and tilted her head. "Maybe you'll even have fun."

I smiled and nodded and grasped tightly onto the bedspread. I squeezed and squeezed and squeezed until the skin on my chewed fingertips burned, and then I squeezed some more.

# AFTER

"WE WON'T BE HERE LONG," says my mother. "I just need laundry detergent."

"Why can't I wait in the car?" My mother's won this small battle. I don't want to be out, out where everyone's looking at me. Where everyone wants to talk. Yet here I am.

My mother sighs and shakes her head. "Staying inside is doing stuff to your head."

Since Detective Williams's visit, my mother thinks I'm losing it. She's even threatened to take me to a therapist, but I know she won't. She doesn't believe in them since the divorce—since the marriage counselor failed to save their relationship.

It doesn't matter what she thinks anyway. Staying inside the car has nothing to do with it. Here's the reality: Devin keeps finding me. At least in the car, no one else will be around to see her find me. I know it's not just because I was in her house, poking around in her room. She's in my house, too. Maybe she's everywhere I am. She's haunting me because of what I did. But I can't tell anyone. So now what?

My mother throws her keys into her purse. "If you won't go on your own, you'll come with me." She turns toward me. "What are you going to do when school starts?"

I roll my eyes and open the car door. School is like a hundred years from now. Like a million. I slam the door shut.

My mother glares at me. "Not necessary."

"Neither is making me come with you."

"In your opinion," she says. "Let's go."

It's hot outside, and the humid air presses against me. I sweat as I make my way across the parking lot.

We walk together into Dreyer's Pharmacy and Surgical Supplies. I chew on my nail, grinding at it. I haven't been here since the day Devin stole the lip gloss.

My mother grabs a cart.

"I thought all you needed was laundry detergent," I say.

"Don't be smart," she says. "As long as we're here, there are a few other things, too." She considers me for a moment, then delivers one of her famous lines. "Why don't you poke through cosmetics? Maybe find something fun?" She smiles. Now I glare at her.

"It was just a suggestion," she says. "Do what you want."

"I will," I say. I don't want to look for cosmetics. But I don't want to hang around with my mother either, so I leave her and make my way down another aisle.

I pass by crafts, aspirins, allergy meds, until I hit the magazine stacks. A little kid is sitting on the floor reading something with a caterpillar on the front.

He looks up at me with big brown eyes. "I'm good at word searches," he says. "I like to find things."

"That's great." I'm in no mood for small talk, but

97

I like little kids and I'm good with them. "Did you find any words yet?"

"Yeah," he says, his eyes wide. "I found *bug, ant,* and *butterfly*." His mother is at the other end of the aisle. She looks over at me, and I smile, offering up a small wave. She smiles back, a little more relaxed, and goes back to what she was doing.

"Ooh, butterfly," I say, sitting down next to him. "That's a hard one."

He smiles. "Told you I was good! Want to watch me find more?"

"Sure," I say.

The boy goes back to his puzzle, and I pick up a fashion magazine. I don't know why; it was always Devin's thing, not mine. I flip through the pages of starving, overly made-up women, and remember immediately why I don't read them.

"What's that?" the boy asks.

"Nothing," I say, putting the magazine down on the floor next to me. "Your word search is much more interesting."

He grins. "Yeah, look: *ladybug*!"

"Genius!" I say, smiling at him. His mom walks toward me down the aisle. "What's your name?" she asks.

"Cass," I say. "Cass Kirschner."

"Do you babysit?"

"I do, I—" I love to babysit, but that's my old life. Although sitting here right now, with the little boy, makes me feel lighter than I have in a long time.

"Great," she says. "I'd love to get your number before we leave."

"Lucas," she said, turning to her son. "I'm just running across to the shampoo aisle. I can see you from there. Be a good boy and read your magazine with Cass, okay?" She smiles at me. "You can get to know each other a bit."

"Sure," I say, realizing that I hadn't known the boy's name. I'm not going anywhere anyway.

"Yay!" Lucas says. "You can help me find the rest of the words. Wait—I don't need your help—you just watch."

"Okay," I say. Lucas's mom throws one more smile my way, then walks across to the shampoo aisle.

I watch Lucas work on his puzzle. He sticks his tongue out to the side when he thinks, and it's very cute. No one here except my mother knows who I really am. Knows what happened. For now I'm just Cass, almost tenth-grader, sitting here with a cute little kid in the pharmacy. It's amazing how free I feel when I'm away from everyone I know.

"Oh, really!" says a voice from the next aisle. It's unfamiliar but sounds like a girl my age. She's giggling. She still has things to be happy about. My heart gets going. Is that someone I know? God, I do not want to run into anyone.

I need to see who it is, see if I need to duck out of there. "Hey, Lucas," I say. "Stay here. I just want to peek around the aisle, okay?"

"Uh-huh." He's too engrossed in his puzzle to care.

"You are too funny!" the girl says as I creep toward the end of the aisle.

"You think so, huh?" says another voice. My heart

gets a jolt. I know that second voice. I poke my head around the aisle.

Chad. Devin's Chad. Wearing the green Dreyer's Pharmacy and Surgical Supplies vest with a name tag. I guess good ol' Chad no longer works in produce at the WayMart.

I pull back again behind the shelves of my aisle. My heart gets going, knocking quickly against my chest. I haven't seen Chad since that day, since the day it all happened, and I don't want to.

I peek out again from behind the aisle. The girl isn't from my school either. She's very thin, pretty, with long straight brown hair that comes down to the middle of her back. Her back is arched, likely for optimal cleavage effect, and she's laughing. Chad's giving her his million-dollar smile, the one he flashed over and over at Devin. Every time he smiles, my stomach sinks deeper and deeper inside me. How is he so damn happy? *Why* is he so damn happy?

"Come here," he says to the girl.

"What?" she says. I swear she's batting her eyes.

Chad doesn't wait for her to respond; he just grabs her. He looks around, no doubt for the manager, then pulls her close. He's got her from behind. She's smiling, but his large arm slowly pushes up against her neck, upward toward her chin. For a moment her eyes grow wide, and she stops smiling.

My head starts to spin. Oh, my God. I step backward and accidentally catch Lucas's hand underneath my foot.

"Ouch!" he says. "What'd you do that for?"

"Sorry," I say. I grab onto a nearby shelf. "I didn't realize you were here."

His mother looks up from across the aisle. I offer up a small smile, and she goes back to examining shampoo bottles.

Lucas frowns. "How come you're not watching me do my puzzle?"

"Sorry." I take a look at his hand. I'm steady again. "Are you okay?"

He shrugs. "Yeah. I'm tough."

I force a smile. "Yes, you are." But I'm still thinking about what I just saw. I need to look again.

"Stay right here," I say. "Really, don't move."

"Don't step on me again," he says.

"I won't step on you if you stay right there." I hold up my hand, like I'm taking an oath. "Promise."

Lucas sits back down on the gray industrial carpet and picks up his magazine.

I poke my head out again from behind the shelves. Chad and the girl are gone. Crap. I should be relieved. The last person I want to see, the absolute last, is him. That night was enough. And yet seeing him here with that girl has got my mind going places, bad places.

A hand grabs my shoulder and squeezes. My arms, my legs, everything, feels weak. My body is unsteady, as if I might topple over.

"You usually spy on people in drugstores?" I turn around. Chad is standing beside me, his large hand digging into my shoulder.

# BEFORE

"I CAN'T BELIEVE YOU'RE really wearing that," I whispered. Devin and I were in the backseat of her father's Volvo, on our way to meet Chad and Marcus at the mall. She'd just shown me the satin, baby-pink lacy bra she was wearing under her too-tight top. She also had on a denim jacket—for now. Parent camouflage.

"Why not?" she whispered back. "It's hot."

"Well, for starters," I said, "your shirt is white."

"So?"

"So you can see the bra right through your shirt."

"So?" she said again, grinning this time, her teeth white as ever. She stuck out her chest, much smaller than mine, but at the moment way more prominent in the tight white shirt.

I stared for a moment. I couldn't help it. Her breasts were perfect, round like peaches, and the part of her chest spilling out of her shirt was very white, almost the same color as the shirt.

I looked up, and Devin was staring back at me, her eyebrows raised, a crooked grin stretched across her face. "A picture'll last longer," she said.

"Shut up," I said. My cheeks grew warm. "It's just"—I shook my head—"it's a little much, don't you think?"

She tilted her head to the side. "Really?" she said.

She looked down at her chest, then back at me. Those blue reflective pools stared at me. I turned away. I didn't like what I saw.

"You know what I think, Cass?" she said. "I think that's not the problem."

God, I hated when she did that. The way she saw through me, saw the things I didn't want her to see. The things I didn't want anyone to see.

"You don't even know this guy," I said.

"So what?" she said softly. "In life you meet new people, Cass." She leaned in next to me. "If you're lucky, you meet smoldering hot new people like Chad."

"I hear you girls are going to catch a movie tonight?" said Mr. Rhodes. He smiled at us from the rearview mirror.

"I already told you that, Dad," said Devin.

"All right," he said. "Just making conversation. You don't mind right, Cass?" He winked at me. I loved how he was so happily oblivious. He would likely drop us off, maybe stop at the supermarket for an errand, then head home to have a relaxing gourmet dinner cooked by Mrs. Rhodes, none the wiser to his daughter's plans. "You girls let me know when you need me to pick you up later," he added.

Devin rolled her eyes at me. "Sorry," she mouthed.

I smiled because I didn't mind. I liked Mr. Rhodes. I saw him a lot more than my own father, anyway, and at least he was interested enough to ask. "Thanks, Mr. Rhodes," I said. He smiled at me again but didn't say anything else.

I leaned in close to Devin, so Mr. Rhodes wouldn't

103

hear. "Maybe you should keep your jean jacket on until you decide whether or not you like him." I wasn't fooling anyone. Even though I was skeptical of the Chad/Marcus wonder duo, Devin knew I was really saying: Please, please give me a chance. Don't show up looking so hot that Chad and Marcus both like you. Let me have a chance even if it's with a guy named Marcus who might end up being a total waste of my time, for all we know.

I tugged on the shirt Devin had chosen for me from my closet after I confessed I never went shopping. It was loose enough to cover the rolls, fitted enough to flatter my chest.

"Fair enough," she said. "If I don't like him, the jacket stays on. If I do, it comes off." She ran her fingers through her bangs. "That's the signal, okay?"

By "the signal" she meant that if she didn't like Chad, we'd make some dumb excuse like we left a Bundt cake in the oven, then make a run for it and call her dad to ask him to pick us up. If she liked Chad, Marcus and I would need to find a hard plastic mall bench on which to spend the evening. There was always a signal.

"Don't worry, Cass," she said, leaning back into the seat. "I have a good feeling about this."

"That makes one of us." I was aware of my buzz-kill status. I just couldn't help myself.

Devin was about to open the car door when she stopped. "It'll be okay," she said. She scrunched up her lips, then tilted her head and smiled. She leaned in close again, placed her hand on my knee, and squeezed. It hurt at first, and I squirmed. But she didn't let go. She was no longer smiling, and her eyes were wide, and I knew, I knew so clearly, at least for that moment, that I was her best friend and she still needed me. A warm sensation rushed up my leg and through my body, and suddenly I didn't mind that she was squeezing a little too hard. Because it also meant she was holding on. She was holding on to me.

She smiled again, only slightly. "Trust me, Cass." Her voice was low. It wasn't a big car. "Best friends, right?"

I nodded. "Right." When she let go I felt the imprint of her hand on my knee, solid and binding. It lingered strong and steady, long after we'd left her father's car and made our way into the crowded mall to find the boys.

# AFTER

"I WASN'T SPYING," I tell Chad. My shoulder hurts. I can feel little, sharp prickles where Chad's fingers hold on. Lucas looks up from his magazine.

Chad scowls. "I saw you watching from—hey—" His eyes narrow. "I know you."

Duh. "Please let go," I say. Lucas looks from me to Chad, then back at me again. He's clearly not sure what to make of this.

Chad takes a step backward and releases his grip. "You were friends with her. With that girl, Devin."

I nod. "Yeah," I say. "That was me."

"What's your name again?"

"Cass," I say softly. It's amazing to me that he's forgotten. That he could forget anything about that night.

"Right, Cass—the guitar chick! You and my buddy Marcus—"

"Yes, okay, I said that was me."

"Who's he?" asks Lucas. I'd already forgotten he was there.

"Just someone I know," I say. "It's okay."

Chad shakes his head. "Crazy shit, all of this. You know what I mean?"

"You said a bad word!" says Lucas.

"Do you mind?" I say. But he's right—crazy, yes. Definitely crazy.

"Sorry, kid," says Chad. Lucas nods at him, satisfied.

Chad leans in closer and lowers his voice. "A girl dies and I'm out with her that night. Crazy, crazy shit."

"Yeah, you already said that."

He's still close. "How is Marcus anyway?"

"I don't know," I say. Doesn't *he*?

"No kidding? I thought you guys were—"

"We're not," I say. "Aren't you supposed to be his friend?"

Chad waved his hand dismissively. "Haven't seen the kid in a while—not since right after your friend, well, you know." He rolls his eyes. "Probably freaked out or something. He's totally MIA now." He shrugged. "Whatever."

Marcus is not MIA, at least as far as I'm concerned. Why is he avoiding Chad? I wonder if that's what Marcus wants to tell me—the reason why he wants to talk.

Chad moves in closer. "You know," he says in almost a whisper, "a detective came to my house."

"Really?" I say, probably unconvincingly.

"Yeah," he says. "I thought I was gonna lose it. I mean, a detective?"

He leans forward again. "He asks me all these questions, and I'm like, dude, I don't know what happened. But he keeps asking." He shakes his head. "I had a headache when he left." Chad's already said more to me than he did the entire time we all went out.

"Cops ask questions," I say.

"Yeah, you have no idea. No idea. Man," he says, slamming his hand against the magazine rack. "I never should've gone out with that chick." He's shaking his head.

"Is that your boyfriend?" Lucas is looking up again from his magazine.

"No," I say quickly.

"No way, kid," says Chad, an awkward grin spreading across his face. Even now, even after everything that happened, he's all over the I-don't-date-the-fat-girl thing. One of the many reasons I'd like to punch him.

Adding to that impulse he says, "Devin was a hassle. No offense."

"Right," I say. "Because there's an inoffensive way to take that." I lower my voice. "She's dead, okay? Leave her alone."

"I didn't mean anything by it," he says, getting right in my face. "You're not going to tell anyone I said that?"

Up close I remember how scary he was—how scary he is. Lucas is watching us now, closely, and I don't want to freak him out. I shrug. "Whatever," I say, hoping no one can hear how loudly my heart is beating. "It doesn't matter what you think. Unless—" My voice drops. We never saw Chad again after, well, *after*.

I can smell his Polo aftershave, see the bits of straw-like stubble on his face. "I didn't do anything." He grabs onto my arm and squeezes.

"Ow." I move away from him, trying to free my arm. He holds on.

"What are you saying? That I had something to do with it?"

"I didn't say that." My arm is killing me. Chad is scary, but he's also scared. Maybe he has a reason to be.

"I didn't do anything." He's still holding on to my arm. "You were there that night." He's nodding. His eyes are wide. "With good old Marcus. What were you two doing again?"

"Please, let go," I say, looking over at Lucas. "You're scaring him." He was scaring me.

"Do you kiss and tell?" Chad says, smirking. "Or is there nothing to tell?" He wags his tongue at me.

"Leave me alone."

"Bet you already spoke to the detective? What'd you tell him?"

"Ow, please." My voice is low. I'm hurting, but I don't want to call attention to this.

Chad runs his free hand through his short, spiky hair. "I gotta get into college next year," he says. "This has to go away. It all has to go away."

"Let go of my arm."

"Mom!" Lucas calls, standing up.

Chad lets go and moves backward. "Sorry," he says. "I wasn't trying to—"

"What's your problem?" I whisper to Chad. "It's okay, Lucas," I say. "He's just joking around."

"It's not funny," says Lucas. "You shouldn't use your hands."

"Yeah, I—I don't know what I'm doing." Chad shakes his head.

I rub my arm. I'll have a bruise there tomorrow for sure. "I talked to the detective, too. I told him I don't know anything."

"Yeah, okay," he says. "Whatever. Just, just forget about it. I gotta get back to work."

"I don't like him," says Lucas.

I watch as Chad heads down the aisle. "Me, neither," I say. "Come on, let's finish your word search."

I settle in next to Lucas. We turn back to his puzzle and then it happens. Again. Gusts of sound pound at my ears. The air around me chills and tightens. I can barely breathe. Devin, oh no, Devin, not now. Please *don't*.

"Stop," I say softly. "Please stop it."

"What? What'd I say?" Lucas stares at me, wide-eyed.

"No, it's not you, it's—" I cover my ears and sink down against the shelves. "Oh!"

Chad stops and turns around. "What the hell's going on? You freaking out on me?"

I shake my head again and again. The sound comes in loud, penetrating bursts.

"No," I say, pressing on my ears. She's everywhere. "Please!" I've covered my ears, but my eyes are wide open. I look for her, but I can't see her.

My body shakes; I can't get warm. "I'm sorry. Just please stop!"

And then I know it's not her speaking, because she doesn't speak to me, but in my head, in my mind, I

110

remember her voice. Devin's voice. It's like she wants me to remember. "*Best friends, Cass. Best friends.*" *Where are you, Devin?* I can feel her. Why can't I *see* her?

"Who the hell are you talking to?" says Chad, looking around. His eyes are wide.

Lucas stands up and cries. "Mom," he says. "Mommy!"

His mother rushes down the aisle toward us. I'm kneeling on the floor, Chad standing over me. She grabs her son. "What's wrong with her?" she says, pulling the little boy over to her.

"I don't know!" Chad says, shaking his head. He puts his hands up in front of him and backs away.

"Honey, you need help," says Lucas's mother.

"No, no, I'm fine. I—"

"I'm getting the manager," she says.

"No, please," I say, still holding my head. It pulses, pounding at my temples. I lean over and press my head against my knees. And then I say with more force than I mean to, "Don't!"

Lucas's mom stares at me. Then she grabs her son by the elbow and whisks him off down the aisle. Lucas watches me the whole way, his mouth hanging open. I am ashamed. So, so ashamed. And confused.

Then it's quiet again. I sit, still holding my head. My whole body, shakes. I breathe in and out, in and out, and try to stop the tremors.

Chad squats down. "Did you have a seizure?"

I shake my head.

111

"It's not drugs, right? You don't seem like the type."

"The type?" My head is still swirling, I hold it to steady the world.

"Who were you talking to?"

"What?" I say. Was I talking out loud?

"You were talking to someone." He says it slowly, as if I'm old or mentally impaired.

"What did I say?" I ask.

He shakes his head slowly. "It was kind of messed up. But you were talking to someone." He tilts his head to the side. "Weren't you?"

"Nobody's here, right?"

"Shit, not that I can see."

I'm the only one who can hear Devin. That's what she wants. That's it. Well, that's good, I guess. No one else has to know.

Chad sighs, then shrugs. "You're just another crazy chick." He stands up and shoves his hands into his pockets. "I gotta get back to work."

Chad blows some air out of his lips. He turns around and walks away from me until he's left the aisle and is out of sight and back into his überjock world.

I slump down against the magazine rack. Sweat drips down from my forehead onto my nose. I don't have the energy to wipe it off. My whole body is numb.

What happened to Devin is my fault. Why else would she be haunting me? I know this is true in the deepest, darkest parts of me. After everything we did that night, after everything that was said. I exhale, then let my head drop into my hands.

"Cass? Are you all right?"

Mrs. Rhodes stands above me, a red plastic shopping basket in her hands.

# Before

Devin walked in front of me, head up and searching as though she owned the freaking mall. I wondered what it was like to feel that way. To feel like just by being somewhere you'd made the place important. A place where other people wanted to be. Or at least to think that about yourself. The only time I felt that way was when I played guitar. When I played, the world was mine; it was anything I wanted it to be. But then again I was almost always alone when I played, so it didn't really count.

I noticed guys checking her out as we walked. Everywhere we went they looked at her. She was pretty, but most of them were looking down, checking out below the neck. I noticed them checking me out, too. More like a why-is-*she*-hanging-out-with-that-hot-chick? look. I was used to it, so I bloused my shirt a little over my pants, looked straight ahead, and pretended I didn't feel the burning on the back of my neck.

"I told Chad we'd meet them in front of the movie theater," she said. "We're a little early."

"Want to walk around?"

She shrugged. "Sure."

We wandered toward the food court since it was on the way. It smelled of an enticing combination of Italian and soy sauces.

"I'm starving," I said, even though I wasn't. I was stalling, and Devin knew it, but to my surprise she stopped anyway.

"Do you want to split a hot pretzel?"

"Okay." That had always been our thing. Ever since we'd started coming to the mall together, we were all about the hot pretzels.

She sighed as we walked over to the pretzel vendor. "One, please," I said. "With mustard."

"No mustard," she said.

"We always get mustard."

She turned to me. "I'm trying to save you from mustard breath."

"No one's smelling my breath."

Devin sighed again. "Not with that attitude." She slapped some money onto the counter. "Keep an open mind, and maybe one day someone will want to smell your breath." She flashed me her Devin smile, and I couldn't help but smile back.

"Mustard, please," I said to the vendor. I looked at Devin and raised an eyebrow.

She shook her head.

The vendor handed me the pretzel wrapped in thin paper. "Careful, it's hot," he said.

"Thanks." I poured on some mustard and took a bite. It was warm and salty, and I was immediately more relaxed. I broke it and offered Devin half.

"No, thanks," she said, looking at her phone.

"You said you'd split it with me."

"I'd say a lot of things if it would get you to chill the hell out."

I rolled my eyes and took another bite. "You sure?" I said. "It's really good."

She sighed. "I don't want to have to worry about food in my teeth."

"Okay," I said, realizing that now *I'd* have to worry about food in my teeth. I didn't think the same way as she did anymore. I also knew that if it were a year ago, or, if I were here with Gina and Lizzy instead, it wouldn't matter if I had food in my teeth. It might've even been funny.

Devin looked at her phone again. "Speed it up, Cass."

I took another bite. "Haven't you heard of being fashionably late?"

"That's just rude. Especially the first time you're meeting someone." She put her hand on her hip. "Let's not forget our manners, my dear."

"Oh, oh, crap." A thin yellow trail ran down my shirt.

"Cass!" Devin's eyes flashed with anger. "Look at you!" She threw up her hands. "I told you not to get the mustard."

"It's no big deal," I said, my cheeks warming. "I'll get it out." I licked my napkin and carefully dabbed at my shirt. "See? Almost gone."

"That's really gross," she said. "Whatever. Your shirt, not mine."

The mustard came out but left behind a small blotch of my saliva. I choked down most of the pretzel. "Last piece." I offered it to her.

"So *not* appetizing." She shook her head. "Are you done?"

"Yeah."

"Feel better?"

I nodded, but I was embarrassed all over again. She knew why I'd gotten the pretzel, and I hoped she wouldn't start talking about it with the boys when we saw them. Not that I cared what they thought. I mean I didn't even know them. But still. I didn't want her to say anything.

"Come on," she said. "Let's get there first; that way we can see them coming."

"What difference does that make?"

"If we decide they don't look that good, we can make a run for it."

"You're kidding, right?" I said. "You met Chad. You know what he looks like."

She shrugged. "I know. But he was wearing his WayMart uniform. What if he doesn't look good in street clothes? What if they both have no fashion sense? I don't want to be humiliated." She looked at me, and I knew she was thinking that I didn't have any fashion sense, and now I had a mustard stain on my shirt. The back of my neck grew warm again.

"Let's just go," I said. "Let's get it over with."

Devin shook her head. "At least pretend that you might have fun."

She had no idea, did she? She had no idea that practically everything now was pretend. I should've been in line for an Oscar. Were we even still friends? I didn't know. All I knew was that I really didn't want to be here with her.

"Oh, my God," she said, stopping. She thrust her hand forward into my chest. "I cannot believe it."

"What?" I said.

Devin threw her hands up in the air again. "I cannot *believe* they're here."

Gina and Lizzy were standing side by side, their backs to us, at the counter of the 1950s diner in the food court.

# AFTER

"Cass?" Mrs. Rhodes says again. "Are you okay?" She looks at me but doesn't kneel down. She's not wearing makeup, and her blond hair is up in a ponytail. For the first time I can remember, she's dressed in sweats and sneakers.

"I was just a little dizzy," I say, sucking in some air. "I didn't eat breakfast." I can't believe Mrs. Rhodes has found me like this. Could she possibly know that Devin was here? *Just* here?

She doesn't seem to. "Most important meal of the day." She puts down her basket and reaches out her hand. "Come, I'll help you up."

I want more than anything right now to reach for Mrs. Rhodes's hand—in every possible way. To tell her what's just happened. To tell her what's been happening. To say, You were right about the garden when you buried her. Devin *is* close. You have no idea *how* close.

"No, thanks," I say instead. "I just need to rest for a few minutes." The coarse industrial carpeting is anything but comfortable, but I stay there even though my butt is sore.

She nods and looks down the aisle. Then she turns back toward me. "Are you here alone?"

"No," I say. "My mom needed detergent." Where is my mother? I want to go home.

She nods again. "No doubt she's made it to the cosmetics aisle," she says, forcing a smile.

"Probably," I say, forcing one back. Mrs. Rhodes would never buy her makeup at a pharmacy, but she's too nice to say that.

"Good," she says, sitting down on the floor next to me. "Then we have a chance to talk."

This is exactly what I don't want. "I'm sorry, Mrs. Rhodes. I'm still not feeling that well."

Mrs. Rhodes takes out an energy bar from her basket. "Here," she says. "Eat this."

The last thing I want is to eat. I imagine any food I ingest falling right through the giant hole in my stomach. But I have to take the energy bar. Mrs. Rhodes thinks I'm just lightheaded. I need to play the part.

"Thanks," I say. I pull off the wrapper and take a bite. The bar is dry and brittle—and a poor attempt at chocolate. I force a smile.

"A little better?" she says as I swallow.

I nod.

"Good. Have some more."

I nibble on the bar.

Mrs. Rhodes takes out a small package of seeds from her shopping basket. "Lilacs," she says, smiling. "I'm going to plant them in the garden. Next to the agapanthus."

I nod. "That'll be nice."

"Devin's favorite—of course you know that," she says. She puts the package of seeds back in the shopping basket. "I think, wherever she is, she'll appreciate them." Her lower lips curl up and she wipes at her eyes.

"Yeah," I say. "I'm sure." We sit in silence for what seems like forever. Mrs. Rhodes finally breaks it.

"You've avoided my calls, Cass."

I nod. "I know," I say. "I'm really sorry."

"Why? Why don't you want to talk to me?" She doesn't look angry, just hurt, like a sad kitten.

I shrug. "I don't know," I say, lying.

"We always talked," she says, patting my knee. "Didn't we?" She smiles again, but not with her eyes.

I shrug again. "I guess so," I say. She's right. We talked a lot. And I liked it. I really liked it.

She reaches toward me and clasps my hand. Her hand is cool, soft and smooth. She loops her fingers through mine. "I've always felt close to you, Cass," she says. "Like you were my own daughter." She squeezes my hand. "Still like you're my own."

This makes my insides curdle. My mind is jumbled, and I search for something else to say. Something that isn't what she wants me to say or what I want to say. I want so badly to tell her what I know, to end this all now, but I can't. I just can't. It's too late. I've gone too far the wrong way.

"You can talk to me, Cass," she says. "Even though"—her voice begins to tremble—"even though Devin's gone, you and me, we can always talk."

"I know," I say. I wish it were that way. I wish, I wish. But the longer I don't tell what happened between Devin and me, the harder it is to tell. Everything will change. Everything.

She moves over so that's she's sitting closer to me. "I'm sorry about the detective," she says. "He told me what happened."

My cheeks grow warm. "Oh."

"They have to speak with everyone, you know. Explore every lead, turn over all stones, as they say. They have to find out." She takes in a deep breath. "I need them to find out what happened to my daughter." Her eyes blur with tears. "You can understand that, can't you?" She shakes her head.

"Yes," I say, nodding. "Of course."

"Look," she says. "I asked him to leave you alone for now. I think it's clear you're not able to talk about things. I can certainly understand that."

Mrs. Rhodes is saying those words, and I'm hearing them. But her voice isn't familiar; there's no warmth. The words are only words, so I don't actually believe she means what she's saying.

"No," I say. "It's okay. I got upset. I mean"—I take a deep breath—"I can always speak to the detective again. I just don't think it will help." Ugh, my stomach turns and turns and turns. I wish I could choke those words back down. Every lie I tell, every untrue word, takes me further and further away from the person I was before this all happened.

She nods and stares straight ahead. "Well, then, I suppose that's it," she says. "We keep looking." She leans back against the shelves, and again we sit for what seems like way too long. Words and thoughts swarm around us but fall unsaid on the gray carpet.

Mrs. Rhodes once again breaks the silence.

"Summer reading?" she says, reaching for a magazine on the floor.

It's one of those stupid fashion magazines but not the one I was reading. It must've fallen to the floor when I slumped down against the magazine rack.

Mrs. Rhodes picks it up. "We get this one at the house. Devin loves to . . ." Her eyes grow wide. She holds up the magazine. "Is this what you were reading?"

"No," I say. I hold up the magazine next to me on the floor. "This one's mine."

Mrs. Rhodes isn't listening. She thrusts the magazine in front of me.

"You weren't reading this, Cass?" she says again. "This, right here, where you're sitting?"

"No, really, I—" My heart smacks into my chest. The magazine is open to one of those light, fluffy chick quizzes, the kind I never take. The kind Devin loved. The title? "Is Your Best Friend Keeping a Secret? Ten Clues for Finding Out the Truth."

# BEFORE

"I CAN'T BELIEVE THEY'RE HERE," Devin said for the third time.

Gina and Lizzy were sipping sodas. We hadn't spoken to them in almost six months. Not since the fight to end all fights. The separation. The ceremonial tossing out of the best-friend charms.

"Of course they're here," I said. "What else is there to do on a Saturday night when you can't drive?"

Devin glared in their direction, her eyes ice blue. "They'd better not come over to us," she said. "They'd better not ruin our date."

*Our* date?

"They're definitely not coming over here," I said. "After everything that happened, Lizzy and Gina will probably never speak to us again. Not after you were through with them." A part of me wished they would come over. I think a big part of me wished we were still friends. I missed Gina and Lizzy, but I could never tell that to Devin. Some things, even thoughts, are unforgivable between best friends.

"Don't try to pretend you weren't there, too, Cass." She folded her arms across her chest.

Gina turned around and looked up at the fluorescent pink Cadillac clock that doo-wops on the half-hour. She said something to Lizzy, but they still didn't see us.

"I cannot stand Gina," said Devin. "I hate both of them, but she's the worst."

It's hard to imagine anyone hating Gina Vincenti. "You don't hate her," I said.

"Of course I do," she said. "Don't you?"

I chewed on my nail. I knew what I was supposed to say, but the words refused to budge. "I guess I never really thought about it," I said instead.

"You never thought about it?" said Devin. "After everything that happened you have no opinion on the matter?"

I shrugged. "Well, we're not friends," I said. "But shouldn't hate be reserved for murderers and international terrorists?" I smiled, but it did nothing for the tension.

Devin rolled her eyes. "You know, Cass, sometimes you're not really that funny."

Her comment stung. "Just making a point."

She put her hand on her hip and tilted her head. "I'll bet you wish you were with them at the mall instead of me."

The word jumped out. "No." Maybe I answered too quickly. Sometimes the right answer was wrong when it came out too fast.

Devin nodded slowly. "I get it." She tightened her lips. "You wish you were still friends with them. You don't care how they treated us. How badly they hurt us."

"That's not true." Not entirely. But I didn't feel that wronged. The only thing that felt wrong was that Gina and Lizzy were no longer our friends.

"It is true." Devin's eyes welled up, but I'd seen this before. She was deliberately not blinking so that they would tear.

"I just, it's, well"—I scrunched up my face—"I don't think they said anything that bad." Devin had been the one flinging poison arrows.

"Really?" The fake tears disappeared, and suddenly she smiled. "Okay, so there they are." She nodded in the direction of the diner. "Go hang out with them. It's what you want."

"Devin, come on."

"No, really. I'll just meet the boys on my own. Maybe you'll be right for once, and they'll actually be serial killers. Don't worry: if I see duct tape, I'll scream. Hopefully someone will hear me."

"You're being ridiculous."

"Am I?" she said. She leaned in close. Her breath was hot and angry on my face. "Tell me, Cass. Tell me you hate Gina Vincenti and her stupid sidekick, Lizzy Tanaka."

"Devin . . ."

"*Tell. Me.*"

"Devin, I never said I wanted to hang out with them."

"You didn't have to." She stared at me, her eyes cold and hard. "It's all over that sad, pouting little face of yours. I know how you think. I'm your best friend, or at least I thought I was."

I sighed. "Forget it."

"Say it, Cass. Tell me you hate them."

"Devin, I . . ."

"I knew it," she said. She held her best-friend charm right up to my face. "I guess this means nothing to you."

My heart beat faster. At that moment I had that terrible thought. I thought again about what it would be like if Devin wasn't my friend anymore. If instead of going on bad double "not-dates" with random produce guys, I could be at the diner with Gina and Lizzy ordering black-and-white milkshakes and cheese fries. I could be alone in my room, strumming my guitar as much as I wanted. I couldn't think of an easy way to make that happen. To make her go away. But I wished that I could.

I touched the charm that dangled from my neck. It was impossible for me to leave Devin Rhodes alone.

"Fine," I said. "I hate them." The words tasted tart and bitter at the same time. I was kicking myself for being such a weenie.

Devin looked at me and nodded, but there was no smile. She was still angry. I was weak and shaky, as if I was coming down with something and should be in bed with a soft pillow, a box of tissues, and reality TV.

"Devin," I started to say, but she held up her hand. She reached into the pocket of her jean jacket and pulled out her stolen lip gloss. She put it on, then mashed her lips together, all the while silent.

Two boys were headed our way. One was well-built, not too tall, and was sporting short blond hair and an expensive-looking watch. The other was tall and very thin, in a black knee-length coat and high-top sneakers. He had black curly hair and skin the color of mochaccino. My heart woke up inside my chest—this one was cute, really cute. I couldn't help thinking it. Not that it mattered, for me, at least. The shorter one broke into a smile, wide and ravenous, like a cat about to devour a small, pretty bird. The other one looked less hungry, more distracted, as if he'd rather be anywhere else besides walking toward Devin and me.

"There she is," said the shorter one. "What's up, Devy-dev?"

Devin turned away from me and moved toward them, chest first. Her demeanor changed completely. "Hi, guys," she said, her voice back up to a sparkly princess octave. She slowly peeled off her jean jacket.

Devin leaned in so that the blond one could plant a quick kiss on her cheek. "Chad, Marcus," she said, "this is Cass." She turned toward me. "My best friend."

In the entire white sterility of the mall, there was nothing whiter, nothing more pure, than her smile.

# AFTER

HOW DID THAT MAGAZINE GET THERE? How was it open to that page? My heart thumps hard inside my chest, and my stomach begins to twist into painful knots.

"I wasn't reading that," I say. My voice shakes. Was it Devin? Did Devin leave that open for us to see? My thoughts whirl around inside my head. The slippers, the magazine? How much power do the dead have? How much power does Devin have?

Mrs. Rhodes closes her eyes and breathes in through her nose. Then she opens them and licks her lips. "Cass," she says. She grips my arm in the same place Chad grabbed me. It still hurts from his grasp.

"You're hurting me," I say, exhaling.

She doesn't seem to hear. She's staring at me, still holding on.

"Cass," she says again, "please, is there something you can tell us?" Her words slide out from her lips; I can almost see them as they're coming out. "Anything about that night? No one will be angry with you. I promise. We"—she bites her lip—"we just want to know what happened." Her voice rises into a high whisper.

This Mrs. Rhodes, this broken Mrs. Rhodes, is so far away from the put together, cheerful, charming Mrs. Rhodes I know. From the Mrs. Rhodes that I've wished many times could be my own mother. Or at least I'd wished that my own mother could be more like her. I don't recognize this Mrs. Rhodes. I want to talk to her—I do. But the longer I keep my secret, the harder it is to tell it. How do I do it? How can I tell her I could've stopped it from happening? That if things had gone differently that night, Devin would still be alive? How can I tell her that?

"I don't know," I say, my words rehearsed by now. I stare at the magazine. It's still open to that same page.

She slides down onto the floor beside me, like a balloon losing its air. I stiffen, not sure what to do. Should I get up, put my arm around her? Nothing I can think of seems like the right thing to do. Then again I passed on doing the right thing a long time ago.

"I'm so sorry," she says. "I didn't mean to jump at you like that."

"It's okay," I say.

"No," she says. "It's ridiculous. A magazine, a damn magazine." She picks it up and hurls it across the aisle. It smacks against the metal shelf and lands on the floor.

She turns to me. "Losing your child." Her eyes well up. "Losing *my* child. I go through it over and over in my head, every day, Cass, every day." She licks her lips again. "If there was something I could do to change things, not make the same mistakes. If there was something I could've done . . ."

What is she talking about? Does she think it's her fault? "Don't say that," I say. "I'm sure—"

"We all make mistakes, Cass," she says, looking down at the floor. "Stupid, selfish mistakes."

Somehow I can't picture that. Mrs. Rhodes is about as good as it gets, and I wish I could tell her that. I wish I could tell her that I want my mother to be more like her. Classier, less opinionated, less angry at the world. I wish I could tell her nothing she did would've changed what happened. But I don't.

"Oh," she says, starting to sob again. "My Devin. Oh, oh, I'm sorry."

She pulls her legs up against her chest and folds her arms over her knees. She sobs into her knees, and I know I should do something, put an arm around her, touch her shoulder, but I'm still totally stiff, unable to move.

I think about how weird it is that Chad works here and that Mrs. Rhodes is sitting with me on the floor. Did they pass each other in an aisle? Would they have brushed by one another, neither one knowing their connection to each other? What did Chad do that night after he left the mall, anyway? Where did he end up? I realize that I don't actually know.

Finally she lifts her head. "You know, it's funny," she says, wiping her eyes. She's talking to me, I think, but she's staring straight ahead. "Sometimes," she says, "sometimes I really think she's still here. I almost feel like I can touch her, hear her. Do you?" She laughs, but I know it's a nervous laugh. "Do you ever feel that way?"

My heart slams into my chest at full throttle. "I— I'm not sure what you mean."

"Mr. Rhodes thinks it's too many cocktails." She clamps her lips together, then turns to me. "It's not, though," she says. "I haven't had a drink in weeks. Not since it happened. Can you believe that?" She throws her hands up in the air, then shakes her head. "Listen to me talking to you about cocktails. What's wrong with me?" She leans against the pharmacy shelves. Then she folds her arms over her knees and drops her head down into them.

I want to tell her that everything will be okay. That time will heal all wounds or something trite like that. Only I know it's not true. Nothing will ever be okay, and she won't ever really heal, will she? How can you heal when you've lost so much? Mrs. Rhodes and me, we still have that in common. I sit with her for another moment before I get up to find my mother.

# BEFORE

CHAD HAD HIS ARMS WRAPPED AROUND Devin's middle. His biceps were thick and veiny. It was clear he worked out.

"Not here, Chad," Devin said, giggling. "Everyone can see!" He was nuzzling her neck from behind and flicking his tongue at her, laughing.

"So what?" he asked. He then squeezed her waist and pretended to take a bite out of her neck.

Devin squealed. "Chad!"

Part of me wanted to look over at Marcus. Wanted to see if his cheeks, like mine, were burning holes through his face.

"Hey, get a room, you two," Marcus said. I turned toward him. His cheeks weren't red at all; in fact, he was smiling. Marcus thought he was being funny. God help me. He would be spewing corny jokes all afternoon until my ears bled with boredom.

My cheeks burned even more when he caught me looking at him. He raised his eyebrows and grinned. I turned away, but not before we made eye contact. And in that second it was clear we both knew we were stuck with each other. At least for the next few hours.

"So, what are we seeing?" Devin said, freeing herself from Chad's grip. We were standing at the entrance to the mall theater.

"I don't care," said Chad. "I'm not planning on watching." He grinned with his white teeth, then grabbed Devin back into his grasp. He squeezed her again.

"Ouch," she said this time. She was still smiling but no longer with her eyes. "That hurt."

"Not into rough sex, huh, Dev?" Chad laughed. But then he squeezed her again. She hit him, and for a second I actually saw a flash of anger in Devin, something I didn't usually see—at least when it came to boys. Chad backed off, and she smiled again, wide and flirty, as though it was all part of a game.

I was frankly a little repulsed by the scene and losing my patience by the minute. "Just decide already," I said.

Chad looked at me, did a once-over, then said, "Why? Are you joining us?"

"I—"

"Just kidding, girly," he said.

"My name's Cass."

He shook his head and smiled. "You're the one who plays the guitar, right?"

"Yeah."

"Dude, you need to go electric with that shit. No granola crunchy crap." He let go of Devin and launched into a heavy-metalesque air-guitar solo.

"I'll take that under advisement," I said, rolling my eyes. Chad was a piece of work—a really bad, poorly imagined piece of work.

"Let's just find something to watch," said Devin. "I'm not hanging out in front of the movie theater all day."

"Hell, no," said Chad, still grinning. He was such a meathead, I swear I could almost see flecks of sirloin growing from his scalp. He was getting less cute by the nanosecond.

Chad took out his wallet from the back pocket of his jeans and pushed some money at the ticket agent. "Two for *Burning Rubber*," he said. "You don't mind hanging back, big guy, do you?" Chad patted Marcus on the back.

The warmth from my cheeks spread to the back of my neck. Marcus and I were not even asked to join. I didn't even like Marcus, but suddenly I felt bad for him. Bad for us. "Nah, you guys go," Marcus said. He dug his hands into the pockets of his coat. "Cass and I will have ourselves a good time out here." He smiled at Chad but didn't even look at me. He knew he was lying.

"Yeah, that's right," said Chad. "Come on, Devy-dev." He grabbed her again, this time around the neck, almost into a headlock. His bicep nearly covered the bottom portion of her face. Her eyes widened for a moment, then she pulled him off of her.

"Seriously," she said. "Stop it."

Definitely anger.

She glared at him, and he smiled at her. But his smile quickly dissolved. "Lighten up, Dev," he said. "We're just having some fun."

"I know." Devin shrugged. Her tone was lighter now, almost apologetic. She looked at me, and this time, I wasn't sure what I saw.

"Come on," said Chad. "The previews are the best

135

part." He nudged her. "And the only part we're gonna see."

"Fine," said Devin, but she smiled. Chad put his arm around her, this time like a normal person, and they headed toward the theater doors.

They were almost there when Devin turned around and looked at me again. "Sure you don't want to join us, Cass?"

I hadn't expected this. I wasn't sure what to do. She hadn't invited me to join her in, like, forever. I looked over at Marcus. If I said no, then he'd think it was because I wanted to hang out with him, and I didn't. If I said yes, I'd need full-on rain gear to protect myself from all the saliva that would be flying around. I'd said yes before. It wasn't the right answer.

"I'm okay," I said. I dug my hands into the pockets of my cargo pants. "Go ahead. I'll see you after."

Devin nodded, but she was still looking at me. I saw something there, in her eyes, but I wasn't sure what. Did she *want* me to come with her?

"Let's go, babe," Chad said, pulling her by the shoulder.

Devin still faced me. She reached for her neck and played with her charm. Our best-friend charm. It dangled in her hand, and she ran her fingers over the chain links.

"What's the problem?" Chad said. "Do you want to go in, or what?"

"Yeah," she said, letting the charm fall back onto her chest. She was still focused on me. "Cass, meet us back here at ten?"

I nodded. "Sure."

"Ten, okay?" she said again.

"I told you, I'll be here."

She nodded, her lips tight. "Okay."

She turned away and disappeared into the half-lit darkness of the theater's corridor.

# AFTER

"YOU NEED TO MOVE ON WITH YOUR LIFE," my mother says a few days after the incident at the pharmacy. "You need to get out. You need to do something. Something besides tagging along on trips to the store with me."

"Your idea, not mine." I head toward the living-room couch. My guitar lies on the carpet nearby. I lug it from room to room, like a wooden security blanket, but still, I'm unable to play.

"Look," she says, unpacking some groceries. "I know you're hurting."

Hurting isn't quite the word. Reeling. Loathing. Drowning. All better words.

"Mom," I say, "Devin *just* died." I flop down onto the couch and prop my feet on the armrest. The cool leather feels good against the warmth of my skin.

"Feet down, please."

I groan and move them. My mother sits on the couch next to me. She's forcing me to go to the mall today with Lizzy and Gina. They called the day before and invited me shoe shopping. In my mother's world a new pair of strappy sandals could part the Red Sea.

"Gina and Lizzy are being good friends," she says.

"Don't cut yourself off. Grab onto people who reach out."

She doesn't mean Mrs. Rhodes, of course, even though she's reached out more than anyone. My mother likes Lizzy and Gina. She was more upset than I was when our little foursome broke up. She wasn't happy that I got stuck in Devin's half of the friendship pie.

"You should call that boy," she says. "Maybe he'll meet you there."

Marcus has now called three times, plus shown up at the shivah, plus launched pebbles at my window. Nothing he says will change what happened, what I did. Maybe he even knows that. All I know is that after that night I don't want to think about what I look like to him. I wish I had a giant eraser that could wipe that day clean, and Marcus and I could start over.

"I want to lie on the couch," I say. I would lie on the couch forever if I could, sink into it until I drown in soft animal hide. I have no more energy. I'm moving in slow motion. And I don't want to go out again. I don't want to worry where I'll be when Devin comes back. What will she do next?

"Grab onto them," my mother says again. "The people who reach out to you. This boy. Gina and Lizzy. They're giving you another chance." She raises an eyebrow and mumbles. "They'd still be your friends if it weren't for Devin."

My head throbs, pushing at the back of my eyes. Even dead, Devin can't escape my mother's accusing finger. If my mother only knew what I'd done, she might point her finger at me for a change, poking a hole into my forehead so everyone would know. A scarlet fingerprint. "Let it go, Mom," I say. I roll over onto my side. "Devin's dead, okay? We're not going to be hanging out anymore."

My mother stiffens and sits up straight. "That's not what I meant," she says, her lips curving into a frown. "What happened to Devin is tragic, devastating. Of course it is. And when I think about if it had been you . . ." She closes her eyes and shivers. "It's too much. Too, too much."

It could never have been me. It was always going to be Devin. Always.

A horn honks outside. My mother jumps up and rushes to the door. "They're here," she says, coming back over to the couch. You'd think she was the one going to the mall. She runs her hand through my hair, and her nails gently scratch at my scalp. "This will be good for you," she says. "I promise."

I have no choice but to go with them. When my mother gets an idea in her head, she clamps down with iron jaws and doesn't let go. My face-in-the-couch-cushion solace is no more.

"Whatever." I slowly lift myself off of the couch. It's an effort.

"Come on, Cass," she says heading out of the living room. "Get your things. I'm going outside to say hello to Gina's mom." The screen door slams behind her.

I grab my bag, push open the screen door, and

walk slowly down the small hill in front of my house. It's spotted with patches of daffodils that match the yellow paint on the house. Devin loved those daffodils, but my mother never let me cut any for her. "It'll ruin the line," she always said, but it felt like she just didn't want to give any to Devin.

My mother leans over the sedan parked in our driveway, talking with Mrs. Vincenti. From the back my mother looks like she could be in high school, with her narrow waist, small, heart-shaped butt, and trendy jeans. I tug on the drawstrings of my cargo pants and toss my bag over my shoulder. Clearly I never swam in her half of the gene pool.

"I know it's just terrible," my mother says before she notices me. "I'm so glad the girls asked her to go. She really needs this. I practically had to peel her off the living-room couch." Her voice drops to a whisper. "Won't even play her guitar. She's completely—" She sees me and offers a wide smile. "There's my girl!"

I wave at Mrs. Vincenti, who waves back, her smile less certain than my mother's. She has Gina's puppy-dog eyes, brown and longing. Gina and Lizzy are in the backseat. I open the door, and they shift to make room for me.

"Hey, Cass," says Gina. She reaches over and gives me a quick hug.

"Hi," I say. I chew on my lip. It tastes like vanilla lip balm.

"We're glad you decided to come with us," says Lizzy, pushing her hair behind her ears.

I can see from Lizzy's puckered face that she

knows I don't want to be here. I feel bad. I know I should be grateful that they're trying to take me back. I like Gina and Lizzy; I always did. But going to the mall with them, going shopping—it feels wrong. One more thing that feels completely wrong.

"It must be really hard for you right now," Gina says. She puts her hand on my shoulder. Her pink nail polish is chipped, and her nails look painfully short. I'd forgotten we were nail-biting partners. She stares at me. "How *are* you doing, Cass?"

It's funny how Devin's the one who's dead, but I'm the one everyone's concerned about. Okay, true, no one can ask her, "Devin are you angry that you're dead?" Or, "Are you pissed off that you only had fifteen years on earth?" It seems weird to me, though, that hardly anyone talks about Devin's loss, only mine. They think I'm a victim, too.

I shrug. "The same, I guess."

Gina and Lizzy nod as though they understand. But they have no idea. I let them think what they want.

Mrs. Vincenti starts the engine and backs out of my driveway. My mother waves dramatically, a large smile plastered across her face. Her waving makes me feel as though I'm off to sea in one of those old-fashioned newsreels. I raise my hand, but I don't smile back. She looks disappointed but manages to smile through it.

We get to the mall a few minutes later. The parking lot is filled with cars and Sunday shoppers. An old woman with a walker is being led by a home health-care aide, a busy mom tugs along small noisy children, and a couple holding hands strolls slowly through the busy parking lot. Everything is the same. Devin is dead, but everything is still the same. Everyone else is still connected.

"Should I drop you girls off by the Shoe Stop?" asks Mrs. Vincenti.

"That's good, Mom, thanks," says Gina. She turns to Lizzy and me. "I need a pair of ballet flats for school."

"Yeah, and I'm always good for a new pair of sneakers." Lizzy lifts her leg and wiggles her foot inside a pink, green, and blue high-top. She and Gina look at each other and laugh.

I'm not in on the joke, but I smile because I'm supposed to. I guess that Lizzy must have a sneaker fetish or something like that, but I'm not sure. It's one of those best-friend jokes. The kind no one thinks is funny except your best friend. The kind of joke I can't tell anymore.

"All right, here we are." Mrs. Vincenti double-parks in front of the store. "Have a good time," she says.

"Thanks for the ride," I mumble, awkwardly.

"See you, Mrs. Vincenti," says Lizzy, hopping out the car door on the other side.

"Bye, Mom," says Gina.

I'm about to get out of the car when Gina rests her hand on my leg. She looks at me closely, examines me, I think, and it seems as though she's about to speak. I wait for her words, my own words creeping up through my throat, ready to jump, maybe, take the plunge, fall where they may—depending upon what she says.

Gina doesn't speak. Instead she squeezes my knee. It's a friendly gesture, a loving one, even, and unexpected. Or, I think, maybe she knows. My joints stiffen. Maybe somehow Gina *knows*. Blood rushes through me, and my body heats up. Gina's hand is still on my knee, still there waiting. What is she doing? What does she want?

And then I remember, and then I realize. My throat clamps shut, and I suck in a sliver of air. Gina's hand on my knee reminds me of when Devin did the same thing to me that day. In her dad's car, when we last went to the mall. My knee throbs, and my heart screams. I yank my leg away.

"Cass?" Gina says. I grab my bag and run out of the car. Sweat soaks my forehead. I don't look back.

# BeFORe

MARCUS AND I WERE SITTING on a hard, plastic mall bench. It was near the movie theater, so we had a good view of the entrance in case Devin and Chad came out, flushed and red-faced and full of lame excuses.

"So, come here often?" Marcus said.

"Yeah," I said. "Probably too much. I was just here last weekend—" I stopped, surprised to see Marcus was smiling.

"What?" I said.

"Nothing," he said. "I was kidding. You know, 'Come here often?' It's a line," he said. "A cheesy one, I'll admit."

"Oh," I said. Marcus *was* actually kind of funny, which made him not a complete ass, as I'd previously suspected. But the adventure had just begun.

"It's okay," he said. "You don't have to laugh or anything."

"I'm not," I said, but now I kind of was laughing. Inside only.

"Yeah, I know." He was smiling, and he had a nice smile. I liked the way his top two front teeth slightly crisscrossed over each other.

"You like video games?" he said.

"Video games?" I made a face. "Uh, *no.*" Then I

145

smiled, a little. I even felt brave. "Your first line was better."

He closed his eyes and brought his arms up to his chest. "Ow, that hurt." He leaned forward again, still smiling. "Didn't think you were a gamer girl. Most girls aren't."

I shook my head, sighed, and tried not to smile. "How many girls have you asked about the video games?" I said. Brave was one thing, but I was pushing it now. I wanted to reach back into the air and grab back my words. But they'd left my sphere of gravity and floated into his. Point of no return.

"All of them," he said. He leaned forward and clasped his hands in front of him.

"How many is that?" I asked. "Girls, I mean."

"Have you met Chad?" he said.

"Unfortunately."

"It's a lot of girls," he said. "A lot of double dates where I'm left with splinters in my ass from these benches."

"The benches are plastic," I said, trying to sound irritated. But my heart might actually have been smiling. I'd met my hard-plastic-bench-warming twin.

"Got me on a technicality," he said. "I exaggerate sometimes." He leaned closer. "So, what else do you want to know about me?"

I leaned back. "What makes you think I want to know anything about you?"

"Well, we're here, aren't we?" he said. "What else are we going to do?" He sat back up. "Come on, ask me something, anything."

"Okay," I said. I thought for a moment. I wasn't used to making small talk with boys. I wasn't used to making small talk at all.

"Do you like sports?" I said, and then thought, *Could I be any lamer?*

Marcus didn't seem to mind. In fact he was still smiling. He shrugged. "I play the occasional pickup hoops game." He sat up and pushed at the air, as if he was making a basket. "You know, *swish*."

I nodded. "Sounds fun," I said, although it didn't. I was terrible at sports, but I pretended to like them because if you didn't, you got accused of having bad school spirit.

"Not so much," said Marcus. "But with my height, what else am I going to do?"

My heart dinged again. We both pretended to like sports. Another point for Marcus. No, maybe two— that was a big one.

Marcus leaned back onto the bench. "So, no real calluses from the guitar, huh?"

Was he looking at my hands? I brought them onto my lap and squeezed them together.

He was looking at my hands, and now he was looking at me.

"I use a pick," I said. "You know, at least with my right hand." I pressed my left hand against the bench. I wasn't ready for him to see the calluses I did have.

"Oh, yeah." He squeezed three fingers together and gave the heavy metal sign. "Like this, right?"

"Something like that," I said, trying not to let my inside grin take over my entire face. Marcus liked music, too. The point tally was rising, like, Everest high.

"So what else?" he said. "Ask me something else."

I didn't want to ask anything too personal, anything that could be taken the wrong way. "How long have you and Chad been friends?" I finally said.

"Forever," said Marcus. "Day care. Side-by-side cribs or something like that."

"Really?" I said. "Wow."

"Yeah, I stole his Binky, and he beat the crap out of me." He grinned. "Things haven't changed much since then, minus the Binky."

"You're kidding, I hope."

"Eh." He shrugged but smiled again.

"He seriously beats you up?"

"Sometimes," said Marcus. "Not as much as he beats on other people. You know guys like Chad. They throw their weight around to prove a point. Just part of the pecking order. I accept that."

"I wouldn't," I said.

"Really?" He looked at me, right in the eyes. "Okay. How about you and little-miss-headlights?"

"Who?" I said.

"You know, your friend's headlights are on, but I think she likes it that way."

It took me a minute to realize he was talking about Devin's shirt. Well, what was protruding from underneath Devin's shirt.

I shifted over on the bench. "You're disgusting."

He gave me a "Who, me?" grin and shrugged. "Hey, guys notice these things."

I folded my arms over my own chest and prayed that I wouldn't get cold. Mine would be more like searchlights.

"Don't worry," he said, which I thought made things even worse, because I'd been ridiculously obvious. "Your shirt's fine." He looked over at me quickly, then turned his eyes toward the marble floor. "It's nice."

I felt warm all over. Was Marcus flirting with me? Not one guy on any of our not-dates had ever hit on me. I didn't even know what to do with this small revelation, but I liked it.

"Thanks," I said, looking down at my sneakers.

"So how about it?" he said.

"How about what?" I asked.

"What's up with you and Devin?" he said. "You don't seem like you'd be friends."

"You don't seem like you'd be friends with Chad, either."

"We have a symbiotic relationship. He beats the crap out of me, and I let him."

"That's not symbiotic."

"It's something," he said.

I suddenly didn't care that Marcus might have been hitting on me. I didn't like that he was questioning my friendship with Devin. I didn't like that he was saying what everyone else probably thought. "I've been friends with Devin for a long time," I said. "Best friends." Without thinking, I reached for my charm.

He leaned in close. His breath wasn't minty, but there was something fresh, something plain about it that smelled right. "I don't think she's such a good friend."

I leaned away from him. "Really?" I looked at my phone. "You've known me for like a minute."

"Yeah and in that minute you've seemed nice. And Devin, well . . ." He shrugged.

"Well what?" I said.

Marcus moved back and looked down at the floor. He leaned over and rested his head in his hands. "Look, I don't want to start something, okay?"

"Start what?" I began to make mincemeat out of my lip.

"It's just, you seem pretty cool."

A rush of warmth spread up the back of my neck. I waited for the "but." *You seem pretty cool, but . . .* How stupid could I have been? He wasn't flirting with me! The let's-just-be-friends speech was about to hit me like a pie to the face. With extra whipped cream for the fat girl.

"What's your point?" I said, moving over on the bench. Only then did I realize how close we'd been sitting.

He looked up at me. He had nice eyes, dark brown and deep, which was only going to make this hurt more. "Chad's not the nicest guy."

"Shocker," I said. The sarcasm poured out of me. Instant verbal armor.

Marcus wiped his mouth with the back of his hand. "Here's the thing." He looked at me, right at me again and said, "Chad usually asks me along only when the other girl's an oinker."

150

My heart, my stomach, my head, everything inside me curdled. "What?" I said. "What?" I shook my head. "I never even met you."

"That's why I'm telling you," he said. He ran his fingers through his hair. "It's what Devin—it's what your *best friend*—told Chad."

If I'd been smaller, I would have crawled underneath the hard plastic mall bench and flattened myself against the cool marble floor. If I'd been smaller, I would have done that. But I wasn't, was I? Just ask Devin. Just ask my best friend.

# AFTER

"How cute are these?" Gina holds up a leopard ballet flat. They're small and narrow. The kind of shoe that stretches out on anyone who doesn't have an extra-narrow foot, like Gina. I will never wear ballet flats.

"For a safari?" Lizzy snickers. She turns to me, and I flash an obligatory smile. I'm calmer now. I still don't want to be here, but I don't have another way home. There's no chance my mom would come get me. I'm tired and achy, and I wish more than anything that I were back on the living-room couch.

Gina frowns. "They're different, at least," she says, slipping on one flat. "I'm so sick of black."

Lizzy shrugs. "I never wear black," she says, "and I'll never wear a dead animal on my feet."

"It's not *real* leopard." Gina rolls her eyes, but mostly, I think, for effect.

"Synthetic leopard," says Lizzy. "What do you think, Cass. Does it really matter?"

I shrug. "I guess it does to the leopard."

Gina and Lizzy both laugh. Gina's a giggler, and Lizzy's always had a loud, barking laugh. Like a coughing seal.

"There's the Cass I remember," says Lizzy. "Funny in an understated kind of way."

I push some hair behind my ear and actually smile a little. "Thanks, I think."

"You were always funny," says Gina, stepping into the matching ballet flat. "Remember how the four of us used to laugh? I mean, really crack the hell up."

"You did the best impression of Mrs. Frye back in eighth grade." Lizzy snorts. "Devin, is that *rude* or is that *ruuuude*?" She laughs again. "I can't do it justice, Cass—it's all you."

Gina laughs. "Devin would get all up in Mrs. Frye's face. Remember that?"

I nod and smile. "Yeah." I do remember. I remember it a lot. I wonder if Lizzy and Gina laughed like that after we weren't friends anymore. I think of their joke in the car about Lizzy's sneakers, and I decide that they probably do. "Seems like a long time ago," I say.

"Not that long ago," says Gina. She rests her hand on my shoulder. Gina's looking at me again the way she did in the car, as if she can turn me inside out and see what's really going on. My stomach tightens. I'm scared. Really scared. I have to get away from them before they realize I'm hiding something. Shelves of shoes are closing in around me.

"It's weird talking about her when she's gone," Gina says. She's still looking at me. I turn away and stare off at some tacky sneaker display. Gina and Lizzy want to talk about things. Deep things. Why does everyone want to talk?

"We never had a problem with you," says Lizzy. "But you and Devin were a package, so . . ." She shrugs.

My body is still in slow motion. I can't spring myself from this shoe store, ex-best friend purgatory.

"She was so"—Gina looks over again at Lizzy and then back at me—"you know, crazy sometimes. The things she did."

"I heard she started shoplifting," says Lizzy. "Is that true?"

*The music store*, I think. Where's the music store? I could buy some sheet music. For my guitar. If I ever play it again.

"She thought she could get away with anything." Lizzy's still going. "Who cares what happens to anyone else?"

The ice-cream stand. Ice cream always makes me feel better. Rocky Road. But it's far from here and wide open. They'll find me.

"Mean," says Gina. "She could be mean." She bites on her lip. "I'm sorry, Cass. That was mean of me. After what happened to her, God." She shakes her head. "I should stop. No one deserves that."

"But even that night," says Lizzy. "At the mall. Right before, well, you know . . . she was awful to us." She shakes her head. "She was awful to *you*, Cass."

Her words spin around inside my head, whirling and twisting. They know. They were there, almost. I need—*need*—to get out of here.

"It's just the way it was," says Lizzy. "We didn't want to live like that. Always feeling bad about ourselves because of things Devin said or did. Just wasn't worth it."

"She wasn't always like that—I mean, there was

154

good in her, too," says Gina. "We know that. It's, well, that last fight." She exhales and shakes her head. "She said some horrible things."

"I mean, who says things like that?" says Lizzy. "Seriously, who does?"

"Even still," Gina says. "We tried to help her that night. She seemed to be spiraling, you know what I mean?"

Spiraling, yeah. Yeah, she was, that night.

"Probably because you were with a guy and she wasn't," says Lizzy. "Whatever happened to him? Are you guys dating?"

I should probably be upset and offended, as any normal person would be in response to the bashing of her dead best friend. Only I don't feel any of those things. I even want to agree with them, a little.

"No," I say. "We're not dating. And it wasn't like that with Devin." I don't even know how to explain what it was like.

"Oh, Cass," says Gina. She looks over at Lizzy again, and then back at me. "Don't take this the wrong way, but you've always been a little blind when it comes to Devin."

"Things were different between Devin and me." I'm not lying, just leaving out compelling details.

Gina looks quickly over at Lizzy. She runs her fingers through her hair. "I know there were good times, too."

"There were," I say. It's true—a little bit true, anyway.

I remember the food court. I should go there. It's big, crowded. I can lose them there. I can get lost.

"You're a good person, Cass," Gina says. "You deserved better."

"Definitely," says Lizzy.

I swallow hard. "I have to go."

"Cass, no." Gina's puppy-dog eyes grow wide.

Lizzy keeps talking. "It's terrible and all," she says, "but I'm not surprised this happened. I mean, if it was going to happen, it was going to happen to Devin." She shakes her head. "It's a good thing you weren't with her," she says. "It could've been you, too."

I back away from them. "I really have to go." I can't let them know. I can't let them know what happened when I was with her.

Gina moves toward me. "Stay, please."

"No, really, I—"

"We're just talking, Cass," said Lizzy.

I continue to back away from them. I really need to get out of here.

Gina grabs my arm. "I'm sorry. We didn't want—"

"What's wrong with you two?" I say. "She's dead!"

I run out of the shoe store and head to the food court. Gina and Lizzy call after me, maybe even chase me, although Gina's still wearing the leopard ballet flats and she'd never shoplift, even by accident. The mall is crowded, and I lose them by the electric neon food court.

The scent of coffee blends with fast-food pizza and hamburgers. It fills my nostrils, souring in my stomach. I lean against a white marble support beam and breathe and breathe and breathe. Gina's words rush in circles through my mind. *You deserved better.*

I deserved better? *I* deserved better? I'm not the one they found that morning at the bottom of Woodacre Ravine. Didn't Devin deserve better? Wouldn't anyone?

The corner of the support beam presses into my back. I feel it then, a hand on my shoulder, squeezing—no, clenching hard. I turn around, but no one's there. I twist but can't pull free.

My shoulder aches, throbs, and tiny droplets of sweat bubble up on my forehead.

"Devin?" I say, my heart pumping quickly. I recognize the feel of her touch. "Devin? It's you, isn't it?" My mouth dries up.

The pain in my shoulder eases, and the feeling moves through my hair, this time gentle, soft. There's almost a sadness to the way it runs slowly through the strands a few at a time. I swallow and press my knuckles into wet eyes.

Her hand tenderly pulls at each strand of my hair, as though remembering. Remembering a time long ago. Little girls playing, lying in the grass, weaving flower crowns in the park. My eyes moisten. Silent fingers move from my hair and brush against my cheek. My cheek tingles, and instinctively I turn my face toward the hand. It moves slowly down my cheek, as if trying to wipe away my tears.

I can feel Devin's sadness. Is it because I'm here with them? With Gina and Lizzy? I bring my hand up to my cheek, and we touch as though we really still could. Her hand runs down along my cheek gently and slowly moves toward my neck. Then onto my neck. There's a hard tug on my charm. Unseen fingers grab onto it, then curl around my neck.

"*Devin!*"

The air tightens and grows thin. The bleached whiteness of the mall grays, then darkens.

# BEFORE

MARCUS SHOOK HIS HEAD. "Crap, they always shoot the messenger."

"Only when the messenger's a jackass." I wouldn't look at him. I felt inside out, all turned upside down. I couldn't even think.

"Hey, I'm sorry," Marcus said, leaning toward me. "I just thought you should know."

"I don't believe you anyway," I said. But I did. Of course I did.

Marcus looked wounded, and I was glad. "You don't have to," he said. "If it makes you feel any better, I don't agree."

I didn't answer. My eyes were focused on the large windows of the mall. Cars drove back and forth. People strolled together through the parking lot. Everyone else had somewhere real to be.

"Devin's wrong, totally wrong," he said.

"Whatever," I said. "It doesn't matter." But it did matter. It meant everything that this was how Devin described me. This is how Devin saw me.

"Now who's being a jackass?"

I still wouldn't look at him, but my lips curled downward. My hands reached instinctively for the charm around my neck. I wanted to pull it off, break the chain, throw it onto the cold, marble floor, and be done.

"Okay, fine," said Marcus. "I'd be pissed, too, if I were you. But get over it. Devin's not the only girl in the world. I'm sure you have other friends."

*Had* other friends. "She's supposed to be my best friend." The words barely pushed through my tightened lips. I was still holding on to the chain.

"I know," he said, backing off a little.

We sat in silence for what seemed like forever but was probably only a minute or two. Collapsing worlds had their own sense of time.

Marcus leaned toward me again. I saw him out of the corner of my eye, but mostly I felt him. Felt him close. "Hey," he said softly, "I think you're cool. And you're nice to look at."

"Stop." I wanted to believe him, I really did, but how could I? "We only have to stay here another hour and a half, two hours, tops," I said. "Then we can both go back to our lives and forget this ever happened."

He ran his hand through his hair. "Maybe I don't want to forget I met you."

I stayed focused on the windows, trying to decide if I should just get up and walk away.

"So, you're going to ignore me?" He dug his hands into his pockets.

"Maybe you can disappear for a while."

"And go where?" he said. "I don't have a car."

"We're in a mall," I said. "I'm sure you can find something to do. Go to the arcade, if you're so into video games. Just leave me alone."

"Fine," he said. He stood up and took his hands

out of his pockets. "I'll leave, but I'm going on the record as saying I don't want to."

My stomach twisted around itself. I didn't want him to go either. But I was too embarrassed to have him stay. I wanted to erase the day. Erase it.

"Wait, I have a different idea," he said. He swayed just slightly from side to side. He stuffed his hands back into his pockets. "Maybe we can start over. You know, like we just met."

I didn't answer, but I wished we could, too. I was still staring out the window. All those people coming and going, their lives still in motion.

Marcus sat down again on the bench next to me. He held out his hand. "Marcus Figueroa," he said. "Nice to meet you."

I couldn't help but turn toward him.

I pursed my lips together then reached out my hand. "Cass," I said. We shook, and his hand was a little sweaty, but I didn't mind. I even thought maybe I had made him sweat, which I liked. "So, now what?"

"Now," he said, "let's ditch this piece-of-crap bench."

"What about Chad and Devin?"

He raised his eyebrows. "What about them?" he said. "They left us out here on a bench. A freaking bench. They won't miss us."

I was energized. "Let's get out of here."

"After you," he said.

"Wait a minute," I said. "I thought you couldn't go anywhere without a car." I was smiling now, full on smiling. Maybe even flirting.

161

"There's always somewhere to go," Marcus said. "It's just not as much fun by yourself." He grinned, and I loved it.

"Fine, you decide," I said.

He brought his finger to his forehead and looked up, as though he was thinking hard. "You like ice cream?" he said. "Oh, sorry, I didn't mean—" His eyes grew wide.

I knew he was thinking he'd just asked a fat girl if she liked ice cream. But I did like ice cream, and somehow I didn't mind the question.

"What do *you* think?" I said. Then I just started to laugh, it was all so ridiculous. And then Marcus started to laugh, and I was laughing so much that it was almost weird, but I didn't care.

Marcus offered me his arm, brimming with chivalry. "My lady."

We walked together toward the food court, still laughing. We walked far, far away from the plastic bench.

I brought my hand up to my neck and held the chain between my fingers. Then I let go of the charm. It fell back down onto my neck, cool and comfortable. But I was letting go.

This was how it all started, I think. I was letting go of Devin.

# AFTER

"Is she okay?" Everything is slightly blurred, but I see a tall woman with bright lipstick looking down at me with concern. I blink several times, and the world comes into focus again.

"I think so," says a vaguely familiar voice. I turn away from the woman and look at the other speaker. "Cass?" Marcus is kneeling beside me. Oh, great. He just *happens* to be at the mall, too. Go figure. "You pass out or something?"

I pull myself up to a sitting position on the hard mall floor. "Um, yeah. I guess." I run a hand through my hair and touch my neck. It's sore, but Devin is gone. Again. If she was ever here, that is. But she was, wasn't she? How could she not have been here? Now it's just me, Marcus, and a group of curious onlookers huddled together by the CheezieBurger in the mall food court.

"Sweetie, do you want me to call security?" The woman is still concerned.

"No, I'm fine," I say. My head is throbbing and my heart is pounding, but I can't tell anyone that my dead best friend may have tried to strangle me.

"Come on," says Marcus. "I'll help you up." He holds out his hand.

I'm mortified that Marcus has found me sprawled

on my butt on the mall floor. I stare at him, and everything gets fuzzy again. I grab my forehead and lean over, because now all I can think about is when we last hung out. It always comes back to the night Devin died. I can't move at all now. My other hand stays plastered to the white marble floor.

"You don't look like you're okay," says the woman. "I don't think she's okay," she says to Marcus.

Marcus kneels in front of me, his hand still outstretched. "Cass?" he says. "Can you get up?"

He has no idea, does he? He has no idea what I've done, no idea that he, in his own way, helped.

My jaw is tight, but I force it open. "What are you doing here?" I say. I bring my hand down from my forehead.

"At the mall?" He makes a face. "What else is there to do on a Saturday when you don't drive?"

My mouth cracks into an awkward smile. I have to pretend everything's okay. That I'm happy to see him. He's wearing his long black coat and a Ript Lizyrd concert T-shirt. My white knight in a black trench.

"Okay, that's a start." I think Marcus smiles, but it's hard to tell because it's more of a smirk. "Well, come on." He's still waiting for me to take his hand. He's probably one-hundred-thirty pounds, soaking wet. His arms are about as thick as runt string beans. I can't let him help me up.

"I can get up myself, thanks." And I do, slowly, noticing on my way that my butt is pretty sore, too. All that extra padding didn't even help.

I stand up and the small crowd of onlookers disperses. The freak show is over.

The woman remains and gives me the once-over with big almond eyes. "All right," she says. "But you get straight on home, sweetie. Make sure your mama checks you out."

"I will," I say. "Thanks."

She smiles at me, picks up her shopping bags, and leaves the food court.

I'm left with Marcus. He's taller than I remember him, and thinner, which is weird because it hasn't been that long since I last saw him. He might've gotten a haircut, too. A set of keys dangles from a belt loop on his jeans.

"You want a drink?" he asks. "I can get you a Coke or something."

"Okay." Sugar rush. Definitely need a sugar rush.

I follow Marcus over to CheezieBurger. The neon sign flashes at me, disco-like.

Marcus leans over the counter. "One Coke, one root beer, two cheeseburgers—loaded, a large cheese fry, and a couple of chocolate-chip cookies." He reaches into his back pocket and pulls out a small Velcro wallet. He suddenly turns to me. "Um, did you want something to eat, too?"

He's probably thinking he should feed me. What else does a fat girl do at the mall?

"No, thanks." I'm not that hungry, and there's no way I'd eat fast food in front of him.

Then out of nowhere he says it: "Why are you avoiding me?"

"I'm not," I say.

"Yeah, you are. If I hadn't found you lying on the mall floor, you'd never be here talking to me."

I sigh. "I haven't been feeling that well."

"You can still make a phone call when you don't feel well."

"I know. I'm sorry."

He nods. "You're a mess about Devin." He shrugs. "I get it. I'm—I'm really sorry."

My body stiffens as if it's turning to stone. "Thanks," I say through tightened lips.

Marcus takes a sip of his soda. "You hear about these things happening, and then, out of nowhere, it happens to someone you know." He looks at me quickly, then turns away. "Well, in my case, sort of know."

It doesn't happen if you're there for someone. If you don't wish for it to happen. If you keep them safe.

"Hey, have they found out anything yet?"

"I don't think so," I say. "I mean there's the detective, but I don't really know."

"Yeah, the detective talked to Chad, too. He texted me after—he was pretty freaked out."

"I heard," I say. "I saw Chad at Dreyer's Pharmacy."

Marcus raises his eyebrows. "Yeah? I heard he was working there now. What'd he say?"

"I guess he's pretty worried," I say. It makes me cringe to think about Chad's hand on my shoulder.

Marcus frowns. "He should be."

"Why do you say that?"

Marcus shrugged. "I don't know. Forget it."

"He says you haven't seen him."

Marcus leans back into the bench. "Yeah."

I bite my lip. "Why not?"

"The way he acted that night at the mall." He shakes his head. "I don't know. We've been friends a long time but—" He clasps his hands together, then leans forward again. "Something else happened that night, Cass," he says. "I mean, I know the way things went down with you two."

I stare at him. He doesn't know. Not all of it.

He nods. "I didn't see, and I didn't hear everything, but it was obvious you and Devin had some sort of fight. Am I wrong?"

I shrug. I'm not going there, I'm not. Part of me wants more than anything to tell Marcus what happened between Devin and me. But to tell him how things ended would mean telling him that the choice I made changed everything. How can I tell him? What will he think of me? What will he do? "It's—I can't." I really can't. The words won't come.

"I know it's hard for you to talk about things." He shakes his head. "But I also know there's more. There has to be more."

"Stop," I say. "Just stop."

"No," he says. "I mean—" He takes a deep breath. "Do you think, Chad . . . ?"

"Pushed her into the ravine?" My heart bumps around in my chest. "Do you?" I mean, the way he acted that night, the way he was with the girl in the pharmacy, all over her in a weird, suffocating way. The way he grabbed my arm.

"They had that problem, Devin and Chad. Remember? Maybe because of us?"

"What are you, a detective now?" I say. My words are bullets. I don't mean to be rude, but I need Marcus to stop talking about what happened. I need him to stop thinking about what happened. Because no matter how she ended up in the ravine, I'm the reason it was able to happen. And no one, no one can ever find that out.

"No," he says, looking a little hurt. "It's just, you know, when something like that happens, you try to think of all the possibilities. You never know what you might remember that could help the police." He digs his hands into his pockets.

"I know," I say. "You're not going to figure out what happened. I mean none of us are." If I'd been her friend, like I promised, there'd be nothing to figure out. It just wouldn't have happened.

"Well, of course not," he says. "Not if you don't think about things—try to figure it out. Don't you want to know?" he says. "If that were my friend, I'd have to know. I'd want to beat the crap out of whoever did it."

I take a deep breath and back up. "I just miss her—that's all." My voice is softer.

Marcus nods. "Yeah. I know." He shifts gears, thank God. "So, who're you here with?"

The answer's not as easy as it should be. Gina and Lizzy were looking for me, their calls unanswered on my phone. Who knows where they are now. They could've given up looking for me. Then there's Devin,

168

my dead best friend, who may or may not be here, too, and who may or may not be trying to kill me. The blood starts to churn again in my body.

"I'm here with friends," I say. "I think they're buying shoes." My throat is still raw. I bring my hand up to my neck. Did I scream? I can't remember.

Marcus nods. "Man, I hate shopping. Although I don't think it'd make me faint." He grins and lifts up a high-topped foot. "I've had these babies for two years. The more holes they get, the better I like them."

"I don't really like to shop, either." I say.

"A girl who doesn't like shopping? That's a new one."

I shrug. "I'm not much for stereotypes." I'm trying to stay with him, but my thoughts keep floating back to Devin. I chew on my lip, biting off pulpy flakes of skin. Where is she? What will she do next? Is she watching me now? Is she always watching?

Marcus waves his hand in front of my face. "Hello, Cass?" He looks at me closer. "You sure you're okay? Maybe you did hit your head."

"I'm fine," I say. "Who are you here with?" It's the first thing that comes out of my mouth. Now Marcus thinks I care who he's here with, even though I really don't. At least I don't think I do.

"Just me," he says. "Needed to get out of the house for a while, you know what I mean?"

"Sure," I say, although I'd give anything to be back on the living-room couch.

"Here's your order," says a pimply kid behind the counter. I instinctively touch my face, grateful for my smooth, clear skin.

"Thanks, man," says Marcus. He lifts the tray and turns toward me. "Here, take your soda."

I lift my soda off the tray. "Thanks," I say. I take a long sip, the cold bubbles tearing away the dryness from my throat.

The food court is crowded. It's an obstacle course of little kids, strollers, and high chairs.

"No tables," Marcus says. "I hate this place on the weekend." He scans the food court again. "Come on, over there."

I follow Marcus out of the food court. We look around near the window. The parking lot is as crowded as the food court, and cars jockey for spaces just the way we hunt for seats. A maroon van pushes its way past a line of cars waiting for spots.

Marcus stops in front of one of the mall benches.

"Free bench, cool." He sits down and puts his tray on the bench next to him. "Sit down. I don't bite, re-member?" He opens his bag of food. "Unless you're a cheeseburger." He shoves the burger into his mouth.

I realize that Marcus is trying to joke with me. But I've forgotten how. Nothing seems that funny anymore.

I look out the window again. A motorcycle has cut someone off and won itself a spot. Some people work that way, I guess.

I take my place next to Marcus on the hard plastic mall bench.

# BEFORE

"COME HERE," MARCUS SAID. After a trip to the food court ice-cream stand, we'd left the mall completely. Now we were about two blocks away, in the parking lot of a smaller strip mall. "I want to show you something."

I followed him behind the strip mall into a parking lot with two large overflowing Dumpsters. Apparently the "Garbage-Be-Gone" label was a misnomer. Behind the parking lot was a neighborhood with small cookie-cutter houses, brick and shingle, with small grassy backyards. "Through here," Marcus said. He climbed through a broken spot in the fence, then held out his hand to me from the other side.

"Isn't this trespassing?" I said. And then I thought, God, I am such a colossal dork for even saying that.

"Not if you live here," he said.

I reached for his hand and let him pull me through. We were in a small yard filled with flower bushes, hanging pots, and ceramic planters. "This is your house?"

"Not exactly," he said. "My aunt Marisol lives here, but she watched me after school for a few years while my mom was at work, so it's kind of like I lived here."

"Will she be mad that we're just showing up?" I said. I tugged on my shirt. I wasn't planning on meeting his family anytime soon.

"No," he said. "She wouldn't care anyway, but it just so happens that she's away this week. Visiting my grandma in Sacramento." He grinned. "Won't be home for a few more days."

"Oh," I said. Then I got it. My stomach went all fluttery. "Oh." Marcus was still grinning at me. I wanted more than anything to go into that house with him.

He walked over to the back porch, ducked under a jingly wind chime, and lifted up a worn straw doormat. "Spare key," he said, holding it up. He pulled open a tattered screen door and popped the key into the door behind him. "After you," he said. We walked together into the house.

"Make yourself at home," he said motioning to a plaid loveseat in what was probably the family room. The walls were old and wood-paneled but cozy and covered with paintings.

Marcus noticed me staring. "Watercolor," he said. "My aunt was really into it a few years ago." He pointed to two large planters in the room. "Now she throws pots."

"She throws them?" I looked around the room. "Why?"

Marcus laughed. "No, she throws them, as in makes them. She's a ceramicist. That's how they say it."

My cheeks grew warm. "Oh," I say. "Got it."

"You're cute," he said.

172

I knew my cheeks were bright red. I turned away. "Your aunt sounds cool."

"She is," said Marcus. "Total opposite of my mom."

I checked off another point in the "pro-Marcus" column. My mother thought she was cool, but that was a far cry from actually being cool.

I sank into the couch, and when he wasn't looking, I loosened the string on my cargo pants. After a large Swiss mocha chip cone from the ice-cream shop, I needed the reprieve. I could almost hear the deep red marks on my stomach sighing with grateful relief. I propped myself up against the armrest and brought my knees up to my chest.

"Mind if I join you?" said Marcus. Before I could even answer, he sat down, then stretched his long body across the couch and rested his head against my knees, which sent a virtual lightning bolt through my body. Marcus turned on the TV.

"This show sucks," he said, flipping the channel. He did it again and again, and the channels went by in a blur.

"We could watch a movie," I said.

"We just left a movie," he says.

"But we didn't see it," I said.

"Wait—hold on a sec." He jumped up from the couch. "Be right back."

"Where are you going?"

He turned and grinned, then disappeared down the hallway.

I played with the string of my cargo pants. Where *was* he going? My legs bounced up and down as I sat on the couch. Here I was alone with a boy in his house. Well, sort of his house. What was I thinking? I didn't do things like this. I started to worry that we should head back to the mall. No doubt Devin and Chad were almost done with their movie.

But then my heart got going as Marcus appeared again, holding a guitar.

"My aunt's," he said.

"It's beautiful," I said. Nothing like the beat-up one I used. It was smooth and polished to a golden hue.

He held it out. "Play for me."

"No way," I said. My cheeks grew warm. "I can't." I'd never played in front of a boy before, and I didn't want to start now. Not when things were going so well. What if I got nervous and messed up?

"Sure you can," he said. He moved closer, arms outstretched, the guitar balancing on them.

"Really, Marcus, I'm not that good." I didn't know why I said that, because I was good. Really good, actually.

"If it makes you feel any better," he said, "I'm completely tone deaf. Even if you blow it, I'll still think you rocked the house."

"Oh, fine," I said, reaching for the guitar. I sat down on the couch and slung the strap over my shoulder. "But only for a few minutes, okay?"

"Deal," he said, still grinning. He sat down on the carpet in front of me.

I strummed a few chords—the guitar was nicely tuned. "Your aunt still plays?"

"Yeah, at night, to relax," he said.

I nodded. "Cool." Then I began to play. I started with a few chords and then transitioned to one of my own songs, the song I'd been working on the past few weeks. I'd never played it before for anyone—only the first few lines for Devin. I got really into it, my eyes closed, my fingers found their way across the strings like they always did. For a moment I wasn't there anymore. I was inside the song, its cadence and melody a part of me.

When I was done I opened my eyes and lay the guitar beside me on the couch. Marcus started to clap. His smile was beaming.

"That was awesome," he said. "Especially when you shifted into A minor—really gave the song layers."

"I thought you were tone deaf," I said, my lips curling into a smile.

"I thought you weren't very good."

"Okay, fair enough," I said.

Marcus got up from the floor and moved in next to me on the couch. There was that lightning bolt again. I took in a quick breath.

He smiled and leaned toward me, and I prayed he couldn't hear the blood pumping double-time throughout my body. Marcus slowly unhooked the guitar strap from around my neck and pulled it off over my head, looking at me all the while. Right at me. He placed the guitar gently on the floor.

I chewed on my lip. "So . . . want to watch that movie now?" And as the words came out, I silently kicked myself for being such a complete and utter dork.

Marcus moved in even closer. "I have a better idea." He wrapped his arms around my neck and brought my face toward his.

Then we were kissing. Me and Marcus. Really kissing. And because Marcus was kissing me so hard, I couldn't get enough air, so I pulled away and coughed.

"Sorry," I said, but he nudged my head back down toward his and kept kissing me, slightly more softly.

"You okay?" he said, his lids half-open. I was appalled because I swear I could see my saliva on his lips.

"Yeah," I said. "I'm fine." He knew. He knew I had no idea what I was doing.

"You want me to stop?" he said.

I shook my head. "No." I didn't, but I wished more than ever I'd read some bad romance novels. Or at least the good pages.

"Good," he said. Then, in an amazing feat of acrobatics, Marcus pulled me across him, and my body flopped down right on top of his. Thankfully there was no thud, but I closed my eyes tightly. I didn't even want to imagine an aerial view: my short flabby body engulfing his long, skinny one.

"Ow," I said instinctively, even though he hadn't hurt me. It was a diversionary tactic—lame, but the best I could think of at the moment. I shifted my weight onto one side of him.

"Sorry," he said, looking up. "Should I stop?"

"Just a bad angle," I said, then I kissed him again.

We stayed like that for I don't even know how long, me on top of Marcus, the two of us probing each other's molars.

Even though it was all more complicated than I thought, and definitely less-hygienic, I was enjoying myself. I thought, *Wouldn't it be great if Devin knew where I was? Wouldn't it just be perfect?*

I moved away from Marcus's lips and kissed his neck. I was amazed I even thought to do this, and Marcus responded with a gentle, "Mmmm."

We continued kissing, but now I had Devin on the brain, and I couldn't shake her. She was going to flip out, and I kind of wanted to see that happen. I wanted her to see what I'd done, tell her where I'd been.

I pulled away. "Devin and Chad," I said.

"Cute couple," said Marcus, eyes still closed, kissing my neck. "*Not.*"

"They're probably looking for us."

Marcus lifted his head, eyes still dreamy. "Maybe." He leaned back in to kiss me.

I pulled away again. "Let's go back," I said. My issue was two-fold. I couldn't really leave Devin at the mall—her dad was my ride home. But I really couldn't wait to see the look on her face when she discovered I'd been with Marcus. That the chubby old oinker Cass had actually found herself a man. A cute one, too.

Marcus rolled over and then leaned back on the opposite armrest. He ran his hand through his bangs and sighed. "Okay," he said. "Okay." He sighed again and shook his head. "You're right. We should go back."

I started to get up, but he leaned over quickly and pulled me close. "Marcus, come on, I—" I pulled away again, but he held on tight.

"Glad we started over, Cass," he said. Marcus planted a quick, soft kiss on my lips. It was so light, so gentle, we barely touched, but the feeling reached from his lips and rushed throughout my body.

My eyes were still open, so I saw that Marcus was smiling. I turned around and leaned back into him and let myself smile, too. He wrapped his long arms around my middle easily, and I didn't feel big at all. In Marcus's arms, in fact, I was just the right size.

# AFTER

"I HAVE A CONFESSION TO MAKE," Marcus says, as we sit together on the mall bench by CheezieBurger.

"What's that?" I say.

"I kind of knew you'd be at the mall today. That's why I came."

"What?" I say. "How?"

"I called you again and your mother might've mentioned that you'd be here." He shrugs, palms up.

I sigh. "Of course she did." But for the first time, I'm not actually annoyed with her.

"So what do we do now?" Marcus asks, leaning toward me.

"About what?" I take a sip of my soda.

"About us?" He shrugs. "We could've talked about it that night, but there wasn't really a good time."

"There was the ride home."

"You were pretty quiet," he says.

I nod. "I'll give you that." I was angry then and also confused and still reeling from what had just happened.

"I've thought about you a lot since then," he says.

"You have?" I'd thought about him, too. But mostly I thought about Devin.

"Yeah, I mean, we had a good time." He looks at me, then runs his hand through his hair. "Didn't we?"

"We did."

"Best bench-warming date I ever had." He smiles. "Although things really picked up when we got off the bench."

"Yeah." I laugh, but really it's all wiped out for me, all negated by what happened next. Everything in my life breaks down to before Devin died and after. I don't deserve to have good memories like that.

"How're your songs?" he says, leaning forward. "The ones you were writing?"

I shrug. "I haven't—I'm not. . . ." It seems like so long ago that the guitar was ever anything important to me. That I could ever pick it up without my fingers going numb.

"I get it." He runs his hand through his hair again. It's sticking up a little on top like a rooster, but it doesn't look bad. Actually, he looks great. "I'm, uh, I'm glad I ran into you."

I turn toward Marcus. He's looking at me. Somehow our faces are close, so close I can see hints of stubble poking out from under the coffee hue of his skin. I can even smell the linen scent of laundry detergent.

"Me, too," I say. Despite everything he reminds me of, I really am happy to see him.

"Cool." He smiles and moves his hand toward mine. At first he just rests it there, on top of my hand, but then he grasps my hand and holds on. I feel this small gesture all the way up my arm, to my shoulder, and it wraps around me. Marcus squeezes my hand, then leans toward me.

My heart bumps faster, knocking itself out in my

chest. I try to slow my breath, but it forces its way out.

Marcus pushes my hair behind my ear.

"Please don't," I say. A warm tear trails down the side of my face.

"I'm really glad," he whispers, his breath rushing against my skin. His lips press against my ear, and the blood pumps through my body, hot and deliberate. He whispers again, but so faint I can't hear. Soft, short breaths, another kiss. His nose nuzzles my neck. I lean into him, close my eyes, and exhale. I shouldn't be here, shouldn't be enjoying this when Devin is dead.

But I am. I can't help myself. And I exhale again and again and again.

A figure moves toward us. I see it from the corner of my eye. I pull back.

"What's wrong?" Marcus whispers.

Mr. Cordeau, the jeweler, is walking toward the food court. "I know him," I say. "I don't want him to see us."

"Okay," Marcus says. He leans back.

"He'll probably tell Mrs. Rhodes," I explain.

Mr. Cordeau passes by us, jangly bracelets and all, without seeing us, I think.

"Come here," says Marcus. "Now no one's watching." He turns my face toward him. He smiles, and despite myself, I smile back. He plants a soft whisper of a kiss on my nose, then on my mouth. He leans over and nestles his face into my neck. I relax a little and shrug because it tickles. For the moment we're just Cass and Marcus, two teenagers making out at the mall. I drown in the normalcy of it all.

Marcus's breath grows louder and hotter against my neck. He pushes into me, and I turn toward him. His breath pours out and grows into a long hiss, hard air blowing on me. My heart jumps, almost stops short. I try to pull away from him, but I can't. I don't know why, but I can't move.

And then there's a sound. And it's not his voice. A sound that pushes through me like a vibration. It's a loud, painful, punching at my eardrums. I shrink down and hold my ears, but the sound keeps coming. It's in my head; it's all around, a ribbon of noise, curling around me, tightening.

I want to scream, but my throat is empty. And then the hands, the fingers—I know them—reach for the charm. And I know they always do; they always reach for the charm. A reminder. *Best Friends.* The hands pull at the necklace, which coils around my neck. The air is drying up, almost gone. I suck in a huge burst of it, all that's left, it seems, and I get up and run. Run from the bench. The hands pull at me, then loosen their grip, and I breathe. I struggle, but I breathe.

My own hands press hard against my ears. The sounds won't stop; they buzz inside me over and over. It's like she doesn't want me here. I have no right to be here, not without her. I have no right to be happy.

Maybe Marcus runs after me—I don't know. I can't think; I can only run. I can only run from Devin.

# BeFORe

MARCUS GRABBED MY HAND. "Let's go," he said, and started to run with me across the parking lot between his aunt's house and the strip mall.

I held on to him, still loving the feel of my hand in his. "Where are we going?" I asked.

"Anywhere," he said, still running. "We can go anywhere. Anywhere we can walk—or run, that is." He turned around and grinned at me.

"We should really get back," I said, trying not to sound out of breath. "At some point." I was starting to feel less inclined to go back. I had no interest in the juicy details of Devin's date, because now I had my own juicy details. And I'd rather just think about them. I wanted to stay with Marcus. I really wanted to go anywhere with Marcus.

"We'll get back," said Marcus. "Eventually." He slowed down as we reached the strip mall. The security lights cast an orange glow over the parking lot, its faded parking lines, and potholes. "It's still early. Look," he said, showing me his watch. He had one of those crazy does-everything watches—the kind that tells time all over the world, can be taken scuba diving, and has video games inside. "We still have at least half an hour." He smiled and held his free hand up toward the sky.

"The night is young and so are we. Who said that, anyway? Somebody famous, right?"

I shrugged. "No idea."

"Smart guy, whoever he was."

"Or girl."

"Yeah, okay," he said, smiling. "Now, let's go enjoy the young night."

"Devin will be so mad." As the words came out, I felt lighter. Like, so what if she was mad? I was here with Marcus, outside, at night. The air smelled like summer, humid and warm.

"Yup," said Marcus. "Freaking awesome."

We walked through the strip-mall parking lot into town. My breath slowed; I was glad to no longer be running. Streetlights dotted the mostly empty streets and only a few small windows showed light. The WayMart was still open, of course, and a few restaurants. Every so often a couple walked by or a small group of kids, but mostly we were alone.

"Take that!" Marcus said, tossing an imaginary something at the WayMart, as we walked by.

"Isn't that where you work?" I asked.

"Exactly," he said. "I'm off right now, and I'm out with you, and I just feel like sticking it to the old WayMart."

Marcus knocked into me playfully. I laughed and knocked back into him.

We continued down the street, holding hands, still occasionally knocking hips. When we passed another couple, they smiled at us, as though we were all in some special club, and it warmed me from the inside out. I could get used to this club.

We hit the end of the block and then turned onto Elm, right by Cordeau Jewelers. The sign on the front door said *Closed*, but a light was on in a back window.

"Wow, he works late," I said.

"Who?" said Marcus.

"The man who owns that shop," I said. "Mr. Cordeau. He's friends with Devin's parents." I held up my charm. "It's where I got this."

"Lucky you," he said, grinning.

"Shut up," I said, giving him a gentle whack. Only I could've listened to him talk all night. "I feel bad for him that he has to work so late on a Saturday night."

"Must be a jewelry emergency," said Marcus. "Oh, no," he said raising his voice an octave or two. "Please help, my twenty-karat diamond fell into the fish tank! The betta's trying to mate with it. I just can't go on! Help! Helllllllp!"

"Stop," I said, laughing. "You're so mean!"

"I'm so *not* mean," he said, grinning.

We walked past Mr. Cordeau's shop and turned the corner at Elm onto the next block. There were fewer people there, more closed shops.

Marcus stopped walking. He stared upward. "Look at that sky," he said. "Unbelievable."

I stopped and turned toward him. I put my hand on my hip. "Is that another line?"

"No." He smiled. "I thought we were past that. Do I still need to use lines? If so, let me know. I saved my cheesiest ones."

I laughed. "No, no more lines, please."

"Good," he said. "You saved me from looking

like a total ass. Now," he said, "check out that sky. No clouds at all. Just stars staring back at us. The same stars people saw thousands of years ago. We can still see them. We can still see those same freaking stars. How amazing is that?"

"Pretty amazing." It really was, not that I'd ever thought about it before. I loved that Marcus had.

"Those stars, man, they can see everything. Just imagine being up that high? If they could really see, imagine that. To see everything. To be everywhere at the same time. Amazing."

Marcus let go of my hand. He moved behind me and wrapped his arms around my waist. At first I sucked in my stomach, afraid that even after being with him at his aunt's house, he'd feel the fleshy rolls under my shirt. That he'd feel them and then head for the hills or, in our case, the other side of the strip-mall parking lot.

He didn't run. Instead he nuzzled my neck with his nose, and I felt his warm, soft breath on my back. I leaned into him and exhaled slowly. I put my hands over his. It didn't matter anymore what Marcus might've felt on my stomach, what he might've noticed. Because his arms were still there, wrapped around my waist, and he still liked me. He really liked me. And that, I thought, was truly amazing.

# AFTER

I BURST OUT OF THE MALL into the hot, humid air. She's here. Devin is still here. And I can't tell anyone my best friend is haunting me. That she's angry for what I've done. That she'll never, ever let me be happy again because of what happened between us. Because then they'll know. People are haunted when they're guilty, when they've done something they need to pay for, right? This is payback. This is what I deserve.

The sun presses against me, and I slump forward and get sick. My CheezieBurger soda, along with remnants of my breakfast, splashes onto the stone pavers of the mall entrance and leaves a sour bubbly aftertaste in my mouth.

"Are you all right, dear?" the voice is deep and familiar.

I look up through watery eyes. Mr. Cordeau is standing there, large and friendly, concern etched across his usually merry face.

"Mr. Cordeau," I start to say. But my words get caught. What can I say that won't betray me? I wipe my mouth with my hand.

He pulls out a cloth handkerchief from his shirt pocket, the kind of handkerchief only older people carry. "Let's get you cleaned up," he says gently. He dabs at the corners of my mouth, then carefully wipes across the front. He starts to move toward my shirt, my neck, and chest, which are also soiled. "Oh, well, now, I—" he sputters, and moves his large hand away from my larger chest. "You'd better take care of that." He smiles awkwardly.

"Thanks," I manage to say, and take the soggy hankie. I wipe my shirt, which takes care of the chunks, just not the big brown stain. "I—I'll clean this and get it back to you," I say, holding up the soiled hanky. "I promise."

"No worries, dear," he says. "I've got plenty more." He smiles. "Feeling any better?"

"A little." I'm so grateful for his kindness, for his ordinary gesture, for his making me feel like maybe this is all in my head. I can swallow again.

Mr. Cordeau looks around. "Are you here alone?"

"Not exactly." I tell him how I came with Lizzy and Gina and then ended up finding Marcus. I don't mention Devin.

"So you left all your friends? Even your boyfriend?" says Mr. Cordeau. "I'll bet they're worried about you."

"Marcus is *not* my boyfriend." Maybe, if things were different . . .

"Maybe you should call them now," he says. "You do have your phone?" He stares at me, his expression less soft, as if I'm about to get a lecture.

"I do," I say. I pull it out of my bag to show him. The missed calls and texts glare back at me. I toss it back in. "I'll text them later. I don't feel good."

"I see that," he says. "You haven't had anything to drink, have you?"

"Just a soda—" I stop. "You mean alcohol?" I say. "Of course not!"

He shrugs. "You never know with young people today. Sorry to offend, but it's an honest question. Especially after everything you've been through."

Everything I've been through? He has no idea what I've been through, what I'm going through. He and his clean hankies, his jangly bracelets, and his jolly grin have no idea. "I don't drink," I say, scowling.

Mr. Cordeau leans close. "How about we get you home?" His tone is lighter now.

Home. Yes, that's where I want to be. Where I've always wanted to be, back on the couch. "Yes," I say, momentarily awash with relief. "If it's not too much trouble."

"I wouldn't think of leaving you here," says Mr. Cordeau. "It's never a good idea for a young girl to wander around the mall by herself. And after what happened to poor Devin Rhodes"—he whistles— "well, there's no such thing as being too careful."

I nod, but at the mention of my dead friend, my gratitude evaporates. The thought of a whole car ride with him asking questions about Devin, digging deep, flashes before me. I sense what's left of my Cheezie-Burger soda making for an encore appearance.

"You know what?" I say. "I really am fine. I'll call my mom." I reach into my bag for my phone.

Mr. Cordeau puts his hand on my arm. I look down at that spot, his large hand holding onto my forearm. I look into his eyes, and he relaxes his grip.

"Nonsense," he says. "I'm here and willing to take you home. End of story."

"I . . . well . . ." There's nothing else I can say. I cringe inside. "Okay, thanks."

We head toward the parking lot. I stare at my feet the whole time and try to keep up with Mr. Cordeau's small talk. Praying he doesn't start to dig again.

"Would you look at how this fellow parked?" he says as we pass a motorcycle taking up two spots. "Some people act so entitled. Like the world is theirs to take from it what they wish."

"I know, really," I say.

"You're not like that; I can tell," he says. He smiles at me, but the jolliness isn't there. "You were a good friend to Devin," he says. "Susan always spoke so highly of you."

Mr. Cordeau is a friend of the Rhodeses. He cared about Devin. He's just being nice. I think, too, about how often he spoke with Mrs. Rhodes. It's okay, I tell myself, clenching. Don't be rude. "My mom hates when motorcycles take up a whole spot."

"Yes, yes," says Mr. Cordeau. "They should have cycle parking up front, like they do with bicycles, don't you think?"

"Uh-huh," I pull my bag closer to me. It digs into my shoulder, but I like the feel of it being close.

Mr. Cordeau's white Cadillac is parked a few spaces away from the motorcycle.

"That guy cut someone off when he was parking," I say. Small talk. Stick to the small talk.

Mr. Cordeau looks surprised. "How do you know?" he asks.

"I saw it from the mall window," I say.

He nods. "You're quite observant."

"No," I say, smiling a little. "Just nosy."

He laughs, but it's sort of a weird laugh, and he doesn't smile. "Yes, well, the world is full of impolite drivers. Remember that when you get your license."

"I just want the license," I say. "Then I'll worry about being polite."

Mr. Cordeau chuckles.

I begin to feel Devin's presence around me again. The tingle is cool and constant on my chest where my charm rests. She's still here, following me out of the mall. "Leave me alone," I say under my breath. I'm surprised at the fact that I'm actually angry. After all, she chased me out of the mall, away from Marcus. "Stop already."

"Sorry?" says Mr. Cordeau.

"Nothing," I say, because I know he doesn't feel what I feel, and if I tell him, he'll probably drop me off at a psych ward.

The air around me chills. I squeeze my arms across my chest and the rush of air returns. I cover my ears. "Stop it," I mumble. It's enough. She can't keep doing this. I can't change what happened.

I try to ignore her. I hum quietly to myself to drown her out. She's still there, her presence gnawing at me, but I shake my head over and over, as if by doing so I can shake her free. I swallow several times. I still taste vomit.

"Good thing we're getting you home," says Mr. Cordeau. "You do seem a bit peaked."

I climb into the passenger side of his car. It's very

clean inside and smells like pipe tobacco. I put on my seat belt as Mr. Cordeau gets into the driver's side.

He starts up the engine and pulls out of the parking spot, the giant lot getting smaller and smaller in the distance.

# BEFORE

IT WAS A QUARTER TO ELEVEN when we returned to the movie theater. Devin was pacing, looking at her phone. Her hair was all wild and out of place. Chad wasn't with her.

"Devin?" I said as we got closer. This was a bad idea. As amazing as my night was, I was going to pay for it right now. "Are you okay?" Marcus rested his hand on the small of my back.

"Where the hell have you been?" she said. "I said meet me here at ten o'clock! Can't you tell time?" Her jean jacket was back on and buttoned.

"Sorry," I said. "I lost track of things."

Devin looked at Marcus, then back at me. Her face transformed into a smug, bitter grin. "Oh, I see," she said. "You were too *busy* to worry about your best friend."

"That's not true," I said. But it was. She knew it, and I knew it. My stomach tugged at me.

"Nice, Cass," she said. "You totally bailed on me. For what, a little action?" She stared at Marcus, giving him the up and down with her eyeballs. "With *him*?"

The irony was not lost on me. How many times had she done exactly the same thing to me? My whole body heated up, bubbled with rage. "Yeah, with him," I said. "Surprised?" Having Marcus with me was empowering.

"What's that supposed to mean?" she said, taking a step back.

"All that stuff you said about having a better attitude, putting on makeup, buying new clothes. You're so full of it!" My anger was full-throttle. "You didn't think Marcus would like me. You didn't *want* Marcus to like me."

"Shut up, Cass," she said. "You don't make any sense."

"I guess telling Chad I was an—oh, what's the word?—*oinker* was meant as a compliment?"

Devin's mouth opened, then closed, then opened again—like a trout caught on a hook, gasping for air. She stared at me, then glared at Marcus. He shrugged, palms up.

"That's not exactly what I said." Devin was always so smooth; she wasn't used to getting caught.

I got right up into her face, and she blinked a few times. "What exactly did you say?"

She frowned and looked away. "I was just being realistic," she said. "I mean, I wasn't going to say you were a supermodel. I said good things, too."

"What good things?"

"Like, well, that you play the guitar." She bit on her nail.

"Correction," said Marcus. "She rocks the guitar."

I looked over at him and smiled. He nodded and smiled back. Then I turned back to Devin. "That doesn't come close to making up for the oinker comment."

194

She shook her head. "Stop it," she said. "Just stop it. You have no idea what I've been through. If you did you'd never speak to me this way."

And we were back to Devin, as always. I was so done with her right now, it was all I could do to stop myself from hauling off and slapping her silly. "I seriously doubt that," I said.

"Why did you leave me, Cass?" she said. "You said you'd wait."

"Are you insane, Devin?" I said. "You *told* us to go."

"I did not," she said, shaking her head. "I asked you to come with us. You *chose* to leave." Her voice rose, almost panicked.

She was sort of right. I remembered now how it happened. How she'd looked back at me. But I left because I thought she still wanted me to leave. Mostly.

"Where's Chad?" Marcus said.

Devin was pacing. "We had a fight," she said. "Your friend is a total jerk. But you probably know that. Thanks for the warning."

"You're the one who set this up," Marcus said. "You two looked pretty cozy before the movie."

Devin rolled her eyes. "Yeah, well, that didn't last long."

"What happened?" I said.

"Oh, like you care."

There was that little part of me, dammit, that did care. "What happened?" I said again.

"Forget it," she said. "You wouldn't understand."

"What's that supposed to mean?" I said.

Devin pulled her hair away from her cheek and closed her eyes. There was a long red mark on her cheek.

"What happened?" I said, forgetting myself.

"Chad happened," she said.

"He did that to you?" Marcus said.

Devin sighed. "His hands were everywhere! I couldn't get away from him. He's really strong." She opened her eyes again and looked at me, then Marcus, then me again. "I finally got free and then"—she exhaled—"I left the movie because I couldn't stand it anymore. I couldn't stand *him* anymore."

"You left the movie?" I said.

"I didn't know where to go," she said, shaking her head. "I thought you'd be out here and we'd just go home. I thought you'd *at least* answer my calls and texts."

Now my head hurt. The only time I'd ever left her. "Did he leave, too?" I asked.

"Well the jerk followed me outside and got me up against the back of the mall."

Marcus shook his head. "He probably thought that's what you wanted."

Devin raised her eyebrows, along with her voice. "Yeah, well, after I smacked him in the head, he got the point."

"You smacked Chad in the head?" said Marcus.

"With my phone," she said.

"Ow." Marcus's eyes were wide. "Hey, power to you, Devin. I don't think that's ever happened to him before."

"Well, it should've," she said. She closed her eyes and stomped her foot, looking suddenly much younger, or actually closer to her real age. "Total ass! Look." She rolled up the sleeve of her jacket and held out her arm. It was red.

"Oh, my God," I said.

"It's where he grabbed me," she said, rolling her eyes again.

My heart thumped inside my chest. "Why didn't you call your dad?" I asked, but I realized at once that I was glad she hadn't.

She knew it, too. "What should I have said? Take me home but I don't know where Cass is? I lost her?" She moved closer to me and held up her phone. "See? He's already called—twice—and I didn't answer." She glared at me. "I look out for you, Cass."

"That is so untrue," I said. "You look out for you."

"Oh, really?" she said. "What would your mother say if I told her where you've been?" She held up the phone again. "Maybe I should call my dad now. Tell him to pick us up. Are you ready to go?"

I looked down, then over at Marcus.

"I didn't think so." She stuffed the phone back into her jeans pocket. "Besides, you'd be in it deep if I told them what happened—why I haven't called back," she said. "Especially since it turns out you were hooking up with this loser."

"Hey!" Marcus said.

"Whatever." She sighed. "Okay. I just"—she ran her fingers through her hair—"I didn't know how I was going to get away from him. Cass. . . ."

I moved closer to Devin and I could see her eyes were glossed over with tears. I hadn't seen her like this in so long; she was so much like the old Devin. The one I remembered. The one who needed me but not just as a sidekick. I reached for her; it was the only thing I knew to do, but she pushed me away.

"You said you'd be here," she said. "You promised."

"I didn't promise," I said. "I just said I'd be here. I was a little late—that's all."

"Not a little," she said. "And you did promise." She shoved the best-friend charm in my face. "*This* is how you promised."

My body was warm all over, and I tightened my fists. "You're mad because I actually had a good time for once and you didn't."

"Seriously?" she said, shaking her head. "That's what you think?" She tightened her lips and crossed her arms over her chest. "You are so immature, Cass."

"You left me on a bench," I said. "You do that to me all the time."

"Yeah, well, you weren't there, were you?" Devin shook her head again. Her eyes were red now, red and wet. She wiped her nose, about to say something. I wished I could walk away, but I couldn't.

And then she was no longer looking at me. "Oh, great," she said, her eyes widening. "This is officially the worst day of my life."

I turned around. Lizzy and Gina were headed toward us.

# AFTER

"I'VE BEEN WONDERING HOW YOU'RE DOING," says Mr. Cordeau as we merge onto the highway. I tell him that I live only about ten minutes from the mall, just off the highway. In the neighborhood I used to share with Devin. "After I saw you at the Rhodeses' house," Mr. Cordeau continues, "I thought, well, you must be in so much pain."

God, he's annoying. Why does everyone want to talk? Why won't they just leave me alone? I watch the exit signs. Only three more until my house. At least it's a short ride. "I'm doing okay," I say.

He nods. "Vomiting at the mall doesn't really look like 'okay,'" he says. "Neither does running away from your friends."

I don't like where this is going. "I told you I'm not feeling well," I say. "I probably have a stomach virus."

"Perhaps," he says. "Or maybe you're having trouble dealing with what happened to your friend." He looks over at me. "It would only be natural."

Natural? Nothing about what's happening to me is natural. What happened to Devin wasn't natural. What just happened, what I felt, what I heard, is not, not, not natural! I want to rip off my seat belt and get out of the car. I want to yell at him to stop looking at me, to keep his eyes on the road, and to stop asking me questions I won't answer. But I don't. "Well, yeah," I say. "Of course I'm still upset."

Mr. Cordeau nods again. We ride in silence for a few peaceful minutes. Gas stations and mini-marts line the highway.

But then the side of my face grows warm, that weird animal instinct we all have, and I know that Mr. Cordeau is looking at me again, really looking.

"Maybe," he says, "maybe you even feel a little responsible, hmm?" he says. "Responsible for what happened to Devin?"

All my muscles tighten at once. Warm blood rushes through my body. Too close, Mr. Cordeau. Much. Too. Close. Then I think, Does he know something? Does he? Oh, my God, does he? "No," I say quickly. "No, I didn't—"

"I just mean that sometimes, when someone close to us dies, we feel guilty that we couldn't do more for them. That we couldn't, you know, *save* them." He takes his hand from the steering wheel and rests it on my hand. I stare at it, unable to move. His hand is smooth and manicured, and one of his gold bracelets brushes against my wrist. I am frozen. Totally frozen.

"We all have a little God complex," he says. His hand remains on mine, large and spider-like. Then he squeezes my hand and puts his back on the steering wheel.

My hand is still glued to my leg, immobile, likely oozing clamminess onto my cargo pants. I am stuck in this car, on the highway, too far from my house to walk.

"I guess so," I say, moving over slightly in my seat. Somehow I pry my hand off my leg and stuff it into my bag. I carefully feel around inside for my phone. I'm relieved at the feel of its cool metal surface. "But there's nothing I can do—" I tug on my seatbelt, which feels as though it might suffocate me.

"No, of course not," he says. He keeps driving. The noise of the highway is not nearly enough to drown out Mr. Cordeau. He turns to me again. "Not unless you know something that could help the investigation."

My heart drops into my stomach. "I don't," I say softly.

"But you were with her that night." His eyes narrow, and somehow he continues to drive even thought it seems as though he's been staring at me for hours. "You must've seen *something*."

"I didn't," I say. "I already told everyone." I squeeze my phone inside my bag. I need to feel it, know that it's there.

"Yes," he says. "I suspect they've all been asking. Which makes sense, given that you may have been the last person to see her. Before, well"—he raises an eyebrow—"before it happened."

My heart is pounding at my chest. Let me out, it seems to say. Let me out of this body. Let me go.

"Maybe something will come to you," he says, nodding. "Something you'll remember in time."

My heart practically leaps into my throat and pushes out the words.

"I don't know what happened!" I say. It all tumbles

out at once. "I don't know because I left her. I—I left her there alone. I let it happen." I take a deep breath. "I let her go."

And there it is. I've said it. *I've said it.* My words float in front of me, take on their own shape, coil around me. Even though I left Devin that night, even though what happened was because I left my best friend, because I wasn't there for her, I just don't know. I don't know how she died. Not exactly. I don't even tell him the last part, that last part of the story, I hold on to it, tightly, because that's all that's left. That's really it.

I look at Mr. Cordeau. He's still driving, but he's nodding. He's nodding over and over again in slow motion. He wants information. He's a friend of the Rhodeses; of course he does. He's not going to stop asking me questions. And now he knows more than anyone else. He's not going to stop until he knows exactly what happened. How what I did, the terrible things I said, the awful things I wished for, allowed it to happen. I am trapped.

"Where are we?" I say. I realize then that I haven't been paying attention, but this doesn't look like the way home. When did we get off the highway? There are no mini-marts. No gas stations. Only trees, thick clusters of sharp pines, reaching up toward the darkening sky.

"Oh, I never go anywhere the same way twice," says Mr. Cordeau. His eyes are on the road now; he's looking straight ahead and smiling. "Once again," he says, "very observant girl." He puckers his lips. "I

202

wonder what else she's seen. What else she knows."

I must've bitten my tongue, because I taste blood in my mouth. It stings as I swallow. *Where are we?*

Suddenly I hear Devin. I feel her. The throbbing in my ear, the cool prickly sensation of her touch. Wherever we are, Devin is here. She's with us. Why? Why is she here *now*?

The air slides in and out of my ears with a loud persistent hiss, whirling around in my head. Long fingers stroke my hair, tug on the strands, hard, then even harder. I cover my ears, but the sounds still come, she still pulls at me. Over and over and over. And even though I can't hear her. Even though there are no words. With each tug of my hair, each burst of air that pushes into my ears, I hear it. I hear inside my head: "You know. You *know*."

I cover my ears and shake my head. I try to shake those words loose and let them fall off me like flakes of crazy tumbling to the ground.

*You know what happened, Cass.*

"Devin," I say softly, my eyes closed. "Devin, please. I don't. I'm so sorry." I cover my mouth, still shaking my head, still hearing her.

"What did you say?" says Mr. Cordeau.

"Nothing," I say. He hears me. Of course he hears me; we're in a car. Stuck together in a car.

The words circle inside my head, rise and fall like air, like labored breaths. They're my words, my brain spins them out, but I don't understand. *You know what happened that night, Cass. You know.* "How could I?" I whisper.

203

"How could you what?" says Mr. Cordeau. "You're not making any sense, Cass."

The air is hot on my face; my cheeks burn and my body prickles all over, as if millions of tiny needles are poking at me, trying to force out the truth. Do I? Do I really know?

*Think Cass. Think about that night. What happened?*

Memories—raw, jagged memories—cut through my mind. That night I left Devin. I left her alone because I was angry. I left her alone because I was tired, because I'd found a boy who liked me, because I was done. Because I was done with *her*. I left her alone. How could I know what would happen? I couldn't. I would never. But because I left her, it did. "Devin," I whisper. "Devin, I'm so sorry. I didn't—"

She tugs again, this time at my charm. I bring my hand up. She pulls at it harder, the chain cutting into my neck. Something pushes at the small of my back, something gentle, but firm, pushes at me. Definitely pushes me forward. I open my eyes.

Mr. Cordeau is right—at that moment, something does come to me. The lights, there were lights that night. Across from the mall. The lights I saw from behind the trees. *Car* taillights. Behind the trees where I last saw Devin . . . before she, before . . .

"I want to go home," I say, sitting up straight. My voice is a whisper, so I say it again. "I want to go home. *Now*." I reach into my bag and pull out my phone. But my hands are shaking, so I fumble and then drop the phone onto the floor of the front seat.

"Of course you do," says Mr. Cordeau. "After all, there's no place like home."

I bend over and reach for my phone, but I can't find it on the black-carpeted floor of Mr. Cordeau's car. I feel around, quickly, my hands brushing against the rough carpet, until I catch hold of it underneath my seat.

I grab my phone, but something, something's under it. Something that's cold and hard, small and metal. I squeeze the phone tightly and bring it out from underneath the front seat. And there it is, rescued, like an underwater treasure pulled from a rusted wreck. Rescued from the carpeted blackness of Mr. Cordeau's Cadillac. There it is.

The other half of my charm.

# BEFORE

"WHAT DO YOU TWO WANT?" asked Devin. She moved closer to me. Suddenly we were allies. Or at least she wanted Gina and Lizzy to think that. I guess in her mind, I was still better than they were. She wiped some mascara lines off of her cheeks.

"What happened to you?" asked Gina.

"Yeah, you're a mess," Lizzy says.

"Like it's any of your business," Devin said, crossing her arms over her chest. "Why are you here anyway?"

"Uh, last time I checked," Lizzy said, "the mall was a public place. Open to everyone, you know?"

"Hi, Cass," Gina said, turning to me quickly.

I was just as surprised by her greeting as Devin. Devin stared at me, wide-eyed. I didn't know what to say, so I mumbled, "Hey."

"I'm Marcus," Marcus said, holding up his hand. "And you guys are . . . ?"

"*Not* our friends," said Devin. She grabbed onto my arm. And just like that, we were reconnected. She linked her arm through mine and pulled me close. "Go away," she said to them. "I'm not in the mood."

"We're not in the mood for you, either," said Lizzy, tossing a piece of gum into her mouth. "We just thought you might be in trouble. You don't need to be such a bitch about it."

"How nice of you," Devin said, pulling me even closer. "But you're a little late." She turned back to Marcus and me. "You're all a little late."

"Devin," Gina said. She was always so calm, it was almost impossible to tell when she was upset. When we had the fight, she was still like that—her voice almost didn't change. "Was that you we saw behind the mall?"

Devin blinked a few times. "What are you talking about?" She squeezed my arm.

"We went outside to make a call," said Gina. "It was so loud in here. We saw you with some guy," she said. "It looked like maybe you were having a fight."

"He had his hands on you," said Lizzy. "Look, Gina. Look at her arm."

Devin quickly rolled down the sleeve of her jacket.

"My buddy," said Marcus. "He's kind of a jerk."

Gina and Lizzy looked at him. "But you're not?" Lizzy said, putting her hand on her hip.

"Nope," he said. "Don't let the T-shirt fool you." He looked at me. "Right, Cass?"

I wanted to smile, but my head was spinning. I was standing there, arguing with Devin, when suddenly Gina and Lizzy were there, and they were being friendly, and I was totally and completely confused. "He's not," I said stiffly. I looked down at the floor.

"Whatever you saw, I'm fine," said Devin, but her voice trembled. She waved her free hand in front of her. "Obviously."

"Good for you," said Lizzy. "Let's get out of here," she said to Gina. "I told you this was a bad idea."

Gina ignored her. "Where's the guy now?" she said. "Did he leave?"

"Yeah, where is Chad, anyway?" said Marcus.

"Do I look like I care?" said Devin.

"Well, maybe you don't want to run into him later," said Gina. "We should make sure he left."

"Again," said Devin. "Not really your concern."

"They're right," I said. "What if he's still here? What if he tries to hurt you again?"

"He didn't hurt me, okay?" said Devin.

"He did," I said. "You just showed us."

Devin scowled. "All of you just mind your own business."

"Maybe she wants to run into him," Lizzy said, frowning. She turned to Devin. "You do, don't you? This is just another one of your big scenes. Looking to create drama, as usual." She shook her head. "I don't get you, Devin Rhodes."

"One of the many, many reasons we're not friends," said Devin. She turned to me, "Right, Cass?"

Gina, Lizzy, and Marcus were all looking at me. Devin was, too. It was only four people, but I was completely pulled in a million different directions. I resented—no, I was angry—that Devin had put me in this place. This place where I had to choose, over and over again.

I sucked on my lip. "Let it go, Devin," I finally said. "They're just trying to help."

Devin's eyes flashed with anger. She opened her mouth, then closed it and stared down at the ground. She loosened her grip on my arm.

"Hey, good luck with that one, Cass," said Lizzy. "Come on, Gina." She put her arm on Gina's shoulders, and the two of them started to walk away. Gina turned back one more time and shrugged.

Then Devin, for the first time in forever, actually listened to me. She let go. She let go of my arm. I felt the release in slow motion, like in a movie, where I watched us separate, saw the actual, official act of our friendship ending.

"I knew you were really on their side," she said. Her eyes blinked with fresh tears. "Thanks for nothing." She took a deep breath, then ran off.

# AFTER

THE CHARM SITS IN MY HAND. It's so small, so light, the same as its twin that hangs from my neck. My palm closes around it.

"Lovely little piece," says Mr. Cordeau. He's pulling the car over, off of the road, down a small slope, into the woods. "One of my favorites."

"No," I whisper. I shake my head. "No, no, no." I reach for the car door, but it's locked. I scramble to find the lock, to undo it, to force myself out of the car and take my chances in the tall forest of pine, but I can't get it to work.

"Oh, it's childproof," says Mr. Cordeau. He parks the car and turns off the lights. "Can't be too safe nowadays," he says, that awful smile still etched across his face. "Not that you're a child, my dear. Fifteen already, aren't we?" He reaches toward me, his coarse hand brushing my cheek. "Oh, yes," he says, "quite the young lady you are. Why, you even have a young man now, don't you? Not really the fat ugly duckling, after all."

I pull away from him and hurl myself into the backseat. Mr. Cordeau grabs onto my leg. My hands grab hold of the back car door. I kick out, and even though I can't see, I aim well and kick him in the face.

He groans, loud and angry, and I scramble into the backseat.

Mr. Cordeau has a bloody nose, a trail of red running from his large nostril down his stubbly face. He's wiping it with a surprised, caught-in-headlights look.

"You little bitch," he says, reaching for me with his large hands. "Your friend didn't fight as hard," he says. "Delicate flower that she was. But she tried." His grin is slanted; it cuts his face into a weird diagonal. "She even got herself out of the car, God only knows how."

I hold my bag up. My canvas zippered shield is all that stands between me and Devin's killer. Her real killer. My killer if I can't get out of this car. I push the bag into his face.

He grabs me by the hair, and my head slams into the car door. My forehead burns, and warm blood runs quickly into my eyes. I bring my hand up to my head and feel the spot where it hit the door. It's warm and sticky, and there's a Frankenstein-like gash where there used to be skin. "Devin was much more accommodating," he says. "She told me how you treated her, all the terrible things you said. She came to me willingly, a soft shoulder to cry on. Poor little Devin Rhodes." His eyes grow wide. "You drove her to me."

"No, no, that's not—" I choke as my heart pounds against my chest.

"Yes," he says forcefully. "And then, when I needed *her*, she pushed me away. After all I did for sweet

Devin Rhodes. Sweet Devin Rhodes, so much like her mother. I never meant for her to die. She shouldn't have tried to run away." His expression changes and is at once calm and quizzical. "You can understand that, can't you?" He says this as though we're having a normal conversation and he wants my honest opinion.

"Why?" I say. The word tastes like blood. None of this makes any sense. I just can't wrap my brain around it.

"Pretty little Devin Rhodes," he says. "Susan's precious flower."

My head throbs; my vision begins to blur. "*Mrs. Rhodes?*"

"Yes, *Mrs. Rhodes.*" He sneers. "She walked around like she was too good for me. She knew how I felt about her. I needed answers about Susan. I needed Devin to explain."

"Mrs. Rhodes is married," I say. I press myself against the backseat and search for a quick way out.

"You have a lot to learn, little girl," he says. "Too bad you won't live long enough to learn it."

"No!" My heart explodes inside my chest.

"I knew it would only be a matter of time before you figured out what happened. I can't have you telling everyone, can I?" he says, gripping my arm as I try to pull away.

I have to get out of here. I don't have any more time. This is it. And then I feel it again, feel her again, Devin wraps herself around me. Her breath, warm on

212

my neck, pushes against me. My head turns just slightly, urged on by her invisible touch. My head lowers and then I see it, silver and shining from the floor of the backseat. I see what she's trying to show me. Right next to me. *A tire iron.* Oh, no. Oh, Devin, I think. Oh. Devin.

I reach down quickly and grab the tire iron in my hands. I squeeze it tightly, then bring it down on Mr. Cordeau's head. He falls down into the front seat, his huge body slumping over. The tire iron slides from my fingers.

Mr. Cordeau moans. My own head pounds, but I reach over him and click open the door locks. Then I reach back and open the back door. I'm still bleeding from the gash above my eye. I tumble quietly out the back door and onto the damp grass. My brain thumps inside my skull, and I can't get up. I lie there, looking up at the night sky, at the stars that dot the blackness, and I think, *Is this it?* Will this be the last thing I ever see? Is this the last thing Devin saw, too?

"I'm sorry, Devin," I whisper. The words lift themselves into the humid air. "Devin, I'm sorry. So sorry."

Then I see lights. Red lights, and they're flashing. A police car and a maroon van pull up. The maroon van, I think, from the mall?

"She's by the car!" someone shouts.

"Cordeau's still in there!"

Two men hop out of the maroon van. One I don't know, but the other is Detective Williams. The police car door opens, and two cops come out. And then, despite the red and white flashing lights, everything, at least for me, goes dark.

# BEFORE

I TOOK A QUICK LOOK BACK AT MARCUS and then ran after Devin. I didn't know why, but I needed to catch up with her. What else could I do?

We ran through the almost empty food court. I wasn't used to running, and my heart banged around in my chest, and my lungs tightened and squeezed, trying to get hold of some air. My cargo pants began to slip down, so I grabbed them by the drawstring and held on.

"Come on, Devin," I called to her. If she heard me she didn't act like it. She didn't even turn when I called out to her.

Then, suddenly, I was following her outside the mall, through the revolving door and into the parking lot. It was dark outside, although the mall gave off a neon glow. Bright-white headlights were everywhere. "Stop it already," I called to her. "This isn't safe!"

Devin paused by a red sports car and leaned over, clearly out of breath. She turned toward me. "Stop following me, Cass. Go home. Go home with your boyfriend, or to your mommy. Leave me alone."

"No," I said. "Please, Devin, let's talk about this. It doesn't have to be this way."

"Get lost, Cass," she said. Then she took off again.

I couldn't keep up. I was running out of breath. "How're you going to get home?" I yelled.

"What do you care?"

I realized then—oh, it was so freeing! *I didn't care.* Why had I even chased her out there? This was what I'd wanted all along, wasn't it? To be free of her. To let go. She didn't deserve me.

I slowed down.

Devin turned and saw that I'd stopped running. We were out of the parking lot, down the road from the mall, and it was dark. Darker still since only a small sliver of moon hung in the sky. Devin, still far from me, stopped running, too. Her blond hair reflected the orange hue of a nearby streetlamp. We walked toward each other, like two cowboys at a duel, and I wondered then, even then, if it was for the last time.

"You said you'd always be there for me," she said.

"I was there for you," I said. "For too long."

"You left me," she said. "You were supposed to wait."

"I came right back," I said. "You can't expect me to sit on the bench and wait for you forever. I need to have a life, too."

"That's great, Cass," she said. "Really great. Well, have a good one."

I threw up my hands. "I'm so sick of this," I said. "I'm so sick of you. It's not all about you! Sometimes," I said, "sometimes it's about me!"

"What are you talking about?" she said. "Who else do you think wants to hang out with you? Who

216

else listens to you play your stupid guitar? Who else tries to help you better yourself?"

It would almost have been funny if it wasn't so pathetic. "Gina and Lizzy were my friends. I think maybe they still are."

"They weren't your friends," she said. "They were mine. Notice how they ditched you, too, after our fight?"

"That's because I sided with you."

"Keep telling yourself that." She shook her head and smiled. "Go off with your boyfriend, Cass. Consider yourself lucky you found someone who doesn't mind the fat."

The words tumbled out of me, taking on a shape and a life of their own. "I hate you," I said. "I hate you, Devin Rhodes. You know what? I don't care what happens to you anymore. Go run off—do what you want. I hope you don't come back. *I hope you never come back*!" I took a deep breath. "I never want to see you again!"

Devin stared at me, her self-important smirk gone. She blinked a few times, and I couldn't tell whether her tears were real. "Cass?" she said.

"Devin, I . . ." She was still looking at me, maybe waiting, I thought, to hear what I was going to say to her. What I was going to say to make this all better, like I always did. But this time I didn't. I stopped myself and pushed whatever words were on their way out back in.

The connection between us shattered, like tiny invisible shards of glass falling softly onto the asphalt.

"Cass, I—" She stopped and looked down at the

ground. Then she looked back at me. "Good-bye, Cass." She turned around and kept walking.

Fine, I thought. Fine, let her go. But I watched her. I watched as she walked off into the silent, black night. Then she turned, her eyes lingering on me for a moment, and it looked like she was going to say something. Call out to me. She stared at me, and her whole face softened, and it was as if the anger, the wild anger that had just been there, had disappeared. She offered up just the slightest smile, and I thought she was going to walk back over to me. It will all be okay, I thought. Everything will be okay. But then she didn't. Instead she turned back around and kept walking. I didn't follow her.

I thought about calling out to her. I thought about telling her it wasn't safe. It wasn't safe for her to walk off into the darkness by herself. Even when I saw the hue of red taillights pass slowly by the bank of trees behind which she'd disappeared, I thought about doing that. But it was dark, I was tired, and I was still angry. So I didn't. That's it. *I just didn't.*

So that night, after I caught a bus ride home with Marcus, our hands linked the whole time, and after I ignored Mrs. Rhodes's calls and texts because I didn't feel like having to tell her what happened, and after I climbed under the covers of my bed and thought about what it was like to be with Marcus and what it would be like to be with him again, that night, I slept soundly at first, because I'd stood up to Devin. I'd let Devin know it was no longer all about her. And until things could be that way, we couldn't be friends.

But still, after a few hours, I climbed out of bed and stared out my window and wondered what exactly she was doing. I wondered, after all, where she was. I wondered how she'd gotten home, what she was thinking about. Those stars—those same stars that saw everything—I wondered, did they know? Did they know if she was safe?

When the phone rang in the middle of the night and it was Mrs. Rhodes again, looking for Devin because she still hadn't come home, and my mother was standing in the doorway to my room in her nightgown, clearly annoyed, shaking her head, hand on her hip, I lied. I lied because I knew I'd made a mistake. A huge, crazy, terrible, selfish mistake. I lied and said we went our separate ways at the mall. I lied and said I hadn't seen anything. I lied and said nothing happened.

And when they found her, nineteen hours later, battered and broken at the bottom of Woodacre Ravine, I knew that I had done nothing to stop her from ending up there. I let her go. Because of a stupid fight, because of my stupid silence. I might as well have put her there myself.

# AFTER

THE HOSPITAL ROOM IS A NICE BRIGHT YELLOW, and there's a polka-dotted curtain that separates me from the girl on the other side who had bunion surgery. The bathroom's on my side of the room, which really doesn't seem fair, since bunion girl is on crutches. But life doesn't keep score, I guess.

There's a large bright window across from me, and in the early afternoon, stripes of sunshine paint my bed. Then there are the flowers, so many flowers. From my parents, from Lizzy and Gina, even from Detective Williams. He'd been looking for a break in Devin's case when he'd gotten an anonymous tip two days earlier. Someone had seen a car just like Mr. Cordeau's Cadillac near the ravine the night Devin died. Detective Williams had been following Mr. Cordeau since then. In the chaos of the busy parking lot, he didn't see me get into Cordeau's car. He'd only seen the car pull away. Who knows what would've happened if he hadn't followed the Cadillac from the mall.

But even if Detective Williams hadn't shown up, Devin did. She was reaching for my charm. She was trying to tell me about *him*—about Mr. Cordeau. She tried to save my life. In my collection of hospital-room flowers, there were some from her parents, of course. They brought me lilacs, Devin's favorite.

Debbie the awesome nurse pushes into the room with, yes, more flowers. Orchids, I think. Red and yellow. "These are from a certain young gentleman caller," she says. "I wanted to check and make sure you were decent before I send him in." She's grinning.

Marcus pokes his head into the doorway and smiles.

"Well, now," says the nurse, "I thought I told you to wait outside."

He shrugs. "Sorry," he says. "I'm not too good at following directions."

She shakes her head, and I love the way the beads in her cornrows *click-clack*. I see the smile on the edge of her mouth. She's happy for me that I have a boy visitor, especially since I'd told her I didn't have a boyfriend.

"Somebody's making a liar out of you," she whispers. "Be back soon."

"Hi," says Marcus. He's smiling, too, hands in his pockets.

"Hi," I say.

"Nice digs," he says.

"Thanks," I say. "I'll be out of here tomorrow."

"I heard." He walks toward me. His hands are still in his pockets, and he's dragging a bit, as if he's not sure how close he can get. He doesn't mention the bandage on my head, and I'm grateful. "Um," he says, "can I sit somewhere?"

I laugh because there's only one place to sit. On the chair next to my bed. The one my mom left there when she and my dad went downstairs to get coffee.

The chair's where my mom's been sitting, my father standing at her side, since I arrived two nights before after they found me just outside a wooded area where Cordeau had taken me.

I nod toward the chair. "I think that's the spot."

"I was hoping you'd say that," he says. "So," he says, sitting down, "how're you feeling?"

I shrug. "A little better." Actually much better now. "Thanks for the flowers," I say. "They're really pretty."

He nods. "Yeah, well"—he leans forward—"you know."

I nod and smile. "And not just for that."

"What do you mean?"

"I mean, for looking out for me. Even though I ran away from you."

He clasps his hands in front of him. "Why did you run away?" he asks. "You know, I followed you through the mall until I lost you."

"I can't explain," I say. "Maybe one day—I don't know." Maybe never. How do you explain your dead best friend following you around? How do I explain that I could have never imagined that Mr. Cordeau had anything to do with all this.

"Apparently Mr. Cordeau had it bad for Mrs. Rhodes," Marcus says, solemnly. "It's just so awful. Devin—and you—were dragged into it. He'll be in prison forever."

I nod at Marcus. I don't want to think about Mr. Cordeau. I want to think about Devin. Now that we know what happened. Now that I know she was trying to help me figure out the truth. Now that it's all over, I wonder if she is finally free.

"I met your mom outside the hospital room," he says.

"She's out there?" I ask. Why hasn't she come in? It's so unlike her to stay outside, to not push her way in and get up into everyone's business.

He laughs. "She seems nice."

"That's one word," I say, rolling my eyes.

"Your dad seems cool, too. Quiet, maybe."

"Well, no one gets to say much when my mom's around."

Marcus smiles. "Yeah, I could see that. Hey, your mom, she, uh"—he lowers his voice—"she told me you're going to testify against him. Against Cordeau?"

I nod again.

I can't change what I did, or didn't do. I can't go back and save Devin. But I realize that no matter what I did, what decisions I made, what happened to Devin was not my fault. It wasn't her fault, either. Only one person deserves the blame, and I can do something about that.

"I can stop this from happening to someone else," I say. "To some other Devin."

"That's good," he says. "Really brave of you."

"You'd do the same. Anyone would." Devin was brave, too. After everything that happened, the old Devin, my best friend, came back to help.

And I know now, more than anything, that no matter where she is, Devin has forgiven me. We've forgiven each other. It's what best friends do.

Marcus jumps up. "Be right back, okay?"

I sit up a little. "Where are you going?"

He holds up a finger and grins, then disappears outside the hospital room. A few seconds later he reappears with my guitar. "Your mom said to bring this to you."

I'm about to say I can't, but I stop myself. I want my guitar. I want it more than anything else I've wanted in such a long time. I sit up even more.

He holds it out. "Play for me."

I reach for it and throw the familiar strap around my neck. The guitar rests perfectly on my lap, and I run my hands over its smooth, faded curves. I pluck a few stray notes. It's still tuned, despite the past few weeks of neglect. Then I close my eyes and begin to play. The notes flow from my fingers, warm and deliberate, and I hum softly along with the melody.

Just then a quiet breeze blows through the room. It winds gently through my hair, twisting it slightly, and brushing up against my cheeks. The air warms the space around me, filling me completely. I open my eyes. The gentle wind grazes the pots of flowers, lingering on the lilacs so that the lavender stalks sway just slightly. And then the breeze, which had barely just arrived, quietly passes.

I stop playing and rest the guitar gently on my lap. "Devin," I whisper. Because I know it's her. "Thank you."

The room is still and peaceful. So peaceful. I stare at the lilacs; the breeze has left the faintest scent of them floating in the room. I breathe in deep and touch my charm. It's cool, as it should be, around my neck, where it will stay, where it will remain, for Devin.

Marcus reaches over and puts his hand on mine. He's smiling wide. Instinctively I loop my fingers around his, and our hands rest together on the white cotton hospital-issue blanket. We stay that way, long after the stripes of sunshine on my bed turn to flecks of moonlight and the scent of lilacs has all but faded from the room.

# ACKNOWLEDGMENTS

AT ITS HEART, *Devin Rhodes Is Dead* is about unwavering friendship and the things we do for those we love. I am fortunate to have so much love and friendship in my life.

With deepest gratitude I thank the following people:

First and foremost my parents, Anne and Irving Wolf, for supporting me through it all, forever and always.

The National Association of Elementary School Principals (NAESP) and Mackinac Island Press for honoring *Devin Rhodes Is Dead* with their generous award and for giving my book wings. I am truly grateful for the opportunity.

Julie Ham, my fabulous editor, for her insight, intelligence, kindness, enthusiasm, and patience, and for bolstering me through every step of this process.

Kelly Murphy for the stunning cover art.

Everyone at Charlesbridge for believing in me and bringing my book to life.

The faculty, staff, and student body of Vermont College of Fine Arts, particularly my awe-inspiring advisors: Margaret Bechard, who explained to me that something actually has to happen in a book; Marion Dane Bauer, who taught me concision, heightened my senses, and helped me find a way inside my characters; Tim Wynne-Jones, who forced me to really think about character motivation and plot; and Ellen Howard, for her humor, sage advice, and friendship.

My dear VCFA classmates, The Unreliable Narrators (who are, in fact, most reliable). You took in a stray student and gave me a home. I can't imagine a more wacky, wonderful, and incredibly talented group of women with whom to share my world. You are all my "writer rocks." Special thanks to Teresa Owens Smith, Sarah Tomp, and Sharry Wright, who read early drafts of this novel and, with their brilliance, helped make it shine.

My earliest readers, Felicia Liss Block, who always listened even when my stories were too scary; and Adina Nack, would-be illustrator and professor extraordinaire, with whom I planted my first story seeds while we hid at the top of the staircase at Grandma's house.

My never-weary, always cheerful band of friends/readers, for helping to keep my BIC (Butt In the Chair) and my spirits aloft: Debbi Michiko Florence, Eric Luper, Stacy Hitsky, Jennie Riegler, Dena Weiner, Beverly Marmor, Helen Kampion, Pam Swerdloff, and many others. Whether it was writing advice, pep talks, critiques, or watching my kids so I could write, thank you all for proving that friendship always, always trumps chocolate.

My in-laws, Susan and Gary Kam and sister-in-law, Cindi Thaw, who often watched my boys during the early years so I could finish my degree. My Aunt Susan and Uncle Myron Nack, and cousin Jaime Nack, who were my West Coast cheering section. My brother, Michael, who enabled me to stretch my imagination with our early childhood make-believe.

My grandparents, Sally and George Schneider and Bucky, Molly, and Rose Wolf for their constant and unconditional love. I wish more than anything that you were here to share this with me.

And, lastly, my three greatest joys, my husband, Jason, and my boys, Ben and Zach. You make everything possible. I love you very much.